£3.00

GW01466531

Anglican classics in the Fyfield series

Richard Hooker
Ecclesiastical Polity: Selections

William Law
Selected Writings

Jeremy Taylor
Selected Writings

WILLIAM LAW

Selected Writings

*edited with an introduction
by Janet Louth*

FyfieldBooks

First published in Great Britain 1990 by
Carcanet Press Limited
208-212 Corn Exchange Buildings
Manchester M4 3BQ

Selection and introduction
copyright © 1990 Janet Louth

British Library Cataloguing in Publication Data
Law, William, *1686-1761*
  Selected writings.
  1. Christian life. Anglican authors
  I. Title
  248.483

  ISBN 0-85635-862-2

The publisher acknowledges financial assistance
from the Arts Council of Great Britain

Typeset in 10pt Palatino by Bryan Williamson, Darwen
Printed and bound in England by SRP Ltd, Exeter

Contents

Introduction

William Law's *Serious Call to a Devout and Holy Life* 'will hardly be excelled either for beauty of expression or for justness and depth of thought,' said John Wesley. Tributes to it abound. Anyone inclined to follow the example of Law's Flavia and read 'a book of piety... if it is much commended for style and language' could hardly do better. But its enormous success has put Law's other books rather in the shade. Its immediate predecessor, *A Practical Treatise on Christian Perfection*, is no less powerfully argued and is wonderfully moving. The early controversial works, too, are full of such fire and wit that no one with a taste for that sort of literature should miss them. With some of the later books there is admittedly a difficulty. Law's mystical bent, and his passion for the visionary writings of Jacob Boehme in particular, were viewed with deep suspicion and sometimes downright hostility in an age when a cool rationality was widely regarded as the best approach to life, including religion. Nowadays, there may perhaps be less distrust of an attempt to expound the mysteries of 'inward religion', as it would have been called in the eighteenth century. Nevertheless, sympathy with such things is to a certain extent temperamental; they are not for everybody. Moreover, even for the most sympathetic and attentive of readers, there are passages of bewildering obscurity, in which Law's usual clarity of thought and expression seems to have deserted him. These difficulties cannot be ignored, but they should not be allowed to put anyone off. At the heart of Law's religion is the conviction that God is love, and of this he writes as plainly as could be wished:

> Divine love brought forth all the creation; it kindles all the life of heaven; it is the song of all the angels of God. It has redeemed all the world; it seeks for every sinner upon earth; it embraces all the enemies of God; and from the beginning to the end of time the one work of providence is the one work of love.

William Law was born in King's Cliffe, in Northamptonshire,

in 1686, two years before James II fled into exile at the court of Louis XIV. His father was a grocer and chandler in the village and a man of some standing. He sent his son William to Cambridge, to Emmanuel College. Law obtained his B.A. in 1708, was ordained deacon in 1710 and became a fellow of the college a year later. He was by this time a convinced Jacobite and, although he proceeded to his M.A. in 1712, he was later set back from this status for making his political sympathies all too plain in a speech at his Tripos. The real testing-point came in 1716, following the Jacobite rebellion of the year before, when oaths of loyalty were reimposed. Law was unable to acknowledge George I as king and resigned his fellowship. In other words, he became a Non-Juror, a successor to those who, at the accession of William and Mary, had conscientiously resigned their sees, livings and college fellowships. This made a career in the Church of England or the universities, which were then effectively a part of it, impossible.

Law first came to public notice with his entry into what is known as the Bangorian controversy. Benjamin Hoadly, the Latitudinarian bishop of Bangor, was something of a caricature of an eighteenth-century ecclesiastic, worldly and ambitious, and a determined opponent of the Non-Jurors. His *Preservative against the Principles and Practices of the Non-Jurors* (1716) contained much that was inimical to the High Church party also and his sermon preached before the king on 31st March of the following year, on the text 'My Kingdom is not of this world', provoked a great flood of pamphlets. By far the most effective of these were Law's *Three Letters to the Bishop of Bangor* (1717-19). He leapt upon Hoadly with skill and passion, arguing his case with merciless logic and searing wit. These letters, to which Bishop Hoadly did not see fit to reply, considering their author insufficiently important, were the first, and perhaps the best, of several controversial works. Some of the subject matter may be of limited interest now, but Law's way of dealing with it is not.

In 1723 Law left Cambridge and entered the household of Edward Gibbon, of Lime Grove, Putney, as chaplain and tutor to his son, also an Edward, who was to become the father of the famous historian. When his pupil went up for a second period in Cambridge, to his own college, Law went with him, and he officiated at his marriage in London in 1736. He was held in high regard by all the members of the family, especially by his pupil's sister, Hester, and remained with them until shortly after Edward Gibbon senior died in 1737.

William Law was an intensely private person. There was enough recorded about his life for A.C. Walton to produce in the middle of the last century *Materials for an Adequate Biography of William Law*, but of his inner life Law revealed next to nothing. We know that he had been interested in mystical literature for some time; he had been interested in Malebranche from his undergraduate days. It seems probable that there may be something in the stories told by some Non-Jurors that Law began to take the practice of his religion more seriously around 1720. Be that as it may, there is no doubting the depth of experience and reflection that lies behind *A Practical Treatise on Christian Perfection*, which appeared in 1726. 'The nature and terms of our Christian calling is of that concern as to deserve all our thoughts and is indeed only to be perceived by great seriousness and attention of mind.' He proceeds to expound the demands of that Christian calling and the end to which it brings us: 'a glorious participation of the divine nature'. Unrelenting in his condemnation of worldly concerns, he points us to a better way: 'For what is all the bustle and hurry of the world but dead show, and its greatest agents but dead men, when compared with the state of greatness, that real life, to which the followers of Christ are redeemed?' There is much that makes uncomfortable reading in all this, for Law insists that the perfection to which all Christians are equally called is such that it requires constant mortification and self-denial, not for its own sake, but because without it the common activities and pleasures of this life can so easily take us over.

For it is the love of our body, and too much care of its enjoyments, that makes us too sensible of its demands and subject to its tempers. Whatever we nourish and cherish so far gains an interest in us, and makes us, in the same degree that it has

got our affection. Till therefore religion has entered us into a
state of self-denial, we live in a state that supports the slavery
and corruption of our natures.

Accordingly he condemns undue enjoyment of meals, reading
'vain and impertinent' books and going to the theatre as unfit
for Christians (he had already written on 'The Complete Unlaw-
fulness of the Stage Entertainment', and his arguments are not
so easy to dismiss as might be supposed). Even seemingly innocent diversions must be avoided, 'for as plain and known sins
harden and corrupt, so impertinences and false satisfactions
delude and blind our hearts and render them insensible of our
real misery or true happiness'. *Christian Perfection* was enorm-
ously influential and greatly admired. Walton reports that one
reader sent his servant with an anonymous gift of £1,000, and it
seems to have been this that enabled Law in 1727 to found a
charity school for fourteen girls at King's Cliffe, where his brother
George still lived.

Persuasive and compelling though this treatise was, *A Serious
Call*, published in 1729, was an even greater success; in time it
became one of the classics of English literature and of Western
spirituality. The general aim of the book is much the same as that
of the earlier one, to persuade its readers that

> as all Christians are by their baptism devoted to God, and
> made professors of holiness, so are they all in their several
> callings to live as holy and heavenly persons; doing everything
> in their common life only in such a manner as it may be received
> by God, as a service done to him. For things spiritual and
> temporal, sacred and common, must, like men and angels,
> like heaven and earth, all conspire in the glory of God.

A Serious Call, however, works out the implications of this in
rather more detail than *On Christian Perfection* and about half the
book deals with times and hours of prayer, suggesting a subject
for each, whereas the treatise has only one chapter, a very powerful and moving one, on the necessity of being fervent and constant in prayer. Another feature that *A Serious Call* develops is

the little character sketches that Law introduces into *On Christian Perfection*. There is Eusebius, who 'would be wholly taken up in the cure of souls but that he is busy in studying the old grammarians and would fain reconcile some differences among them before he dies'; or Silvius, who 'laughs at preaching and praying, not because he has any profane principles, or any arguments against religion, but because he happens to have been used to nothing but noise, and hunting, and sports.' In *A Serious Call* there are many characters described in just a few words and also some more detailed portraits, notably of Flavia and Miranda and of Paternus and Eusebia, whom Law uses to set out his ideas on the education of the young of both sexes. It is perhaps inevitable that the sinners, so sharply observed, should be more entertaining to read about than the saints, and Law does not quite succeed in conveying the wonderful attractiveness of true holiness. However, as Mrs Thrale remarked, there is 'prodigious knowledge of the human heart' in these characters and they are very engaging. Although Law insists that 'an exalted piety, high devotion and the religious use of everything is as much the glory and happiness of one state of life as it is of another', he addresses himself chiefly to those with a certain amount of time and money, as he points out elsewhere. There is 'in all orders and conditions...one common holiness', but what we have here is primarily a manual of practical devotion for ladies and gentlemen. Upon such the book made a profound impression. Yet it is so deeply concerned with matters which go beyond mere circumstances that it has long impressed itself on people socially less well-placed. Dr Johnson was one of what was to be a very long line when he said that reading *A Serious Call* was 'the first occasion of his thinking in earnest about religion.' Some of the book's readers came to Putney to seek out the author, among them John and Charles Wesley and John Byrom, the diarist, inventor of a system of shorthand and writer of verses, best known of which is the fine Christmas hymn, 'Christians, Awake!' Byrom became a lifelong friend.

A year before the publication of *A Serious Call*, Law was ordained priest, largely, it seems, to please his fellow Non-Jurors. He was still active among them at this stage, taking part in the liturgical disputes which were then dividing them. From about 1732 his involvement in such things grew less and he turned his attention to other matters. His early interest in mystical theology grew with the years. We know that he admired the work of several of the early Church Fathers, especially Augustine and Dionysius the Areopagite (then still mistakenly regarded as 'apostolical'), the writings of several fourteenth century German mystics, such as John Tauler, and, nearer his own time, Teresa, John of the Cross, Francis of Sales and the French Quietists.

> If a man have no desire but to be of the spirit of the gospel, to obtain all that renovation of life and spirit which alone can make him to be in Christ a new creature, it is a great unhappiness to him to be unacquainted with these writers, or to pass a day without reading something of what they have written.

While Law was still at Putney he came across a writer who was to have more influence on him than any of these, Jacob Boehme (1575-1624), or Behmen, as Law calls him: the works of the seer from Gorlitz in Silesia eventually became almost his only reading. His veneration of Boehme led him into paths where many of his earlier admirers, notably John Wesley, could not follow him.

Soon after the death of the elder Edward Gibbon, Law left Putney and probably spent the next two or three years in lodgings in London. He was once again involved in controversy with Hoadly, this time chiefly on the subject of the Eucharist, of which the bishop had written *A Plain Account*, maintaining that it was a commemorative rite only. Law's reply, *A Demonstration of the Gross and Fundamental Errors of a Late Book*, is a fine display of his powers of argument; it has a great deal to say about the weakness of reason in comparison with the inward instinct of goodness or piety of the heart. There are already some signs of Boehme's influence in the *Demonstration*, but Law's next book, *The Grounds and Reasons of Christian Regeneration* (1739), echoes many of his themes, the fall and its consequences, the wrathful fire of darkness, the necessity for repentance and humility and the rebirth of divine nature in the soul. The book is an excellent introduction to the way in which his thought was developing and avoids most

of Boehme's obscurities and excesses. Several of Law's charac-
teristic ideas which are taken up in later works appear here: that
'God is love, yea, all love, and so all love, that nothing but love
can come from him, and the Christian religion is nothing else
but an open, full manifestation of his universal love towards all
mankind'.   CREATION

It is perhaps not surprising that Law's books should have produced some protest. One of his more outspoken critics, and one
to whom he felt bound to reply, was Joseph Trapp, rector of two
fashionable London churches, author of a play and first Oxford
professor of poetry. The title of Trapp's *Discourse of the Folly, Sin
and Danger of being Righteous overmuch* speaks for itself and Law
gave it *An Earnest and Serious Answer* in 1740. In the same year
he also defended himself against Trapp's attacks on his mystical
writings in his *Animadversions on Dr. Trapp's Late Reply*, vigorously,
as ever, but with a marked degree of restraint in view of the
horrors with which Trapp charged him (malignity of spirit,
shameful ignorance, a blundering mind, nauseous dullness,
ignorance of logic, to mention but a few). That same year, too,
saw the publication of *An Appeal to all who Doubt the Truths of the
Gospel*. It is a remarkable book, full of wonderful rolling passages,
but it is undeniably heavy going and depends very much on
Boehme's somewhat fantastic cosmology, which includes a belief
in an external nature preceding the created world. Indeed, Law's
book begins with a ferocious attack on the traditional doctrine of
creatio ex nihilo, which had been established by the great Athanasius
at the time of the Arian controversies of the early fourth century.

After the publication of these works, nothing more of Law's
appeared for nine years. At the beginning of this period he
returned to his native village of King's Cliffe, to devote himself
to a life of retirement, reflection and works of charity. Three years
later he was joined by the devoted Hester Gibbon and by Mrs
Hutcheson, the widow of an admirer, each of whom had a comfortable private income. The three of them thus adopted the way
of life envisaged by Law in his *Serious Call*:

If therefore persons of either sex, moved with the life of Miranda, and desirous of perfection, should unite themselves into little societies, professing voluntary poverty, virginity, retirement and devotion, living upon bare necessaries, that some might be relieved by their charities, and all be blessed with their prayers and benefited by their example,...such persons... might justly be said to restore that piety, which was the boast and glory of the church when its greatest saints were alive.

The members of the little household assembled to pray and read the Bible together, at the time of the midday meal and at tea-time. They attended all the services at their parish church and twice a week, after the Wednesday and Friday morning service, they rode out, Law and Hester Gibbon on horseback and Mrs Hutcheson in her carriage. At home the women spent much of their time copying out passages of the 'ancient divines'. Walton tells us that 'Mr. Law kept four cows, the produce of which, beyond what was required for his household, he gave to the poor, distributing the milk every morning with his own hands.' There was always a pot of soup on the stove and no one in need was turned away, but was provided with food, clothes or money as required. In fact the liberality of Law and his companions attracted so many hopefuls to King's Cliffe that some villagers began to object and the rector felt moved to protest from the pulpit. He failed to bring about any change. 'Merit is no measure of charity', as Miranda said. Further charitable institutions were added to the girls' school. Mrs Hutcheson founded a school for boys and there were alms houses and a library where works of devotion could be borrowed.

After nine years without publishing anything, Law wrote his *Spirit of Prayer*, *Way to Divine Knowledge* and *Spirit of Love* in rapid succession. The middle one of these was intended as 'preparatory to a new edition of the works of Jacob Behmen and the right use of them', which edition, however, Law never produced. *The Spirit of Prayer* and *The Spirit of Love* are the finest of his later works and display the full development of his mystical thought. Certainly there are places where he gets swept away by his obsession with Boehme (in 1755 John Wesley wrote him a letter full of objections), but the cogency and vigour of his writing and the love that infuses it are very beguiling. Alexander Whyte, who made a study of Law at the end of the last century, wrote of *The Spirit of Love*:

> He sees the unseen roots of things with his own eyes, and he tells us what he sees in his own words, till it may safely be said that no man of a sufficiently open and sufficiently serious mind can read Law on these awful and unfathomable subjects without having his seriousness immensely deepened and his love to God and man for all his days fed to a seraphic flame.

The form of these two books is similar. Each is in two parts, the first straightforward exposition, in two chapters in *The Spirit of Prayer* and in a letter to a friend in *The Spirit of Love*, and the second composed of dialogues (the dialogue form was used in *The Way to Divine Knowledge* too). Theophilus, who represents Law himself, full of a deep and kindly wisdom, though something of a know-all, develops and enlarges on the themes of the first part in response to questions and comments from his friends. It is an effective device, although it is hard to swallow Rusticus, who, we are asked to believe, is entirely without education, and it is difficult not to feel sorry for Humanus, who is there on condition that he does not open his mouth.

In the closing years of his life, Law continued with his writing and engaged in a considerable quantity of correspondence. His last work, *An Address to the Clergy*, was almost ready for the printer at the time of his death. He died on 9 April 1761, from a chill he had caught while auditing the accounts of the schools. Hester Gibbon wrote that 'after taking leave of everybody in the most affecting manner, and declaring the opening of the spirit of love in the soul to be all in all – he expired in divine raptures'.

Leslie Stephen said of *A Serious Call* that it should be read on the knees, and the same could be said of several of Law's other works. But even those determined to remain firmly seated should find something there that cannot easily be ignored. The strength and plainness of most of the writing and the depth of feeling that lies behind it demand attention. When Law says in the introduction to *Christian Regeneration*, 'for the Deists and unbelievers have a great share of my compassionate affections, and I can never think or write of the infinite blessings of the Christian redemption without feeling in my heart an impatient longing to see them the happy partakers of them', there is no doubt that he means it. Reservations there must be, however. Boehme's more amazing theosophical speculations could well have been subjected to some of that critical sharpness that Law applied to the ideas of Hoadly and Trapp. Sometimes his austerity and hatred of this world's more innocent pleasures become repellent. One can understand Mrs Thrale's hesitation when she wrote to Dr Johnson: 'I now half wish I had never followed any precepts but his'.

It should perhaps be mentioned that Law would certainly have disliked the idea of a selection of extracts from his works. 'I only ask this favour of the reader, that he would not pass any censure upon this book, from only dipping into this or that particular part of it, but give it one fair perusal in the order it is written, and then I shall have neither right nor inclination to complain of any judgment he shall think fit to pass upon it,' he wrote in an 'Advertisement to the Reader' at the beginning of the *Appeal*. But this volume is not intended as a basis for a final judgement; it is an introduction, designed to induce readers to proceed further.

The only complete edition of Law is the private reprint of G. Moreton: *The Works of the Revd. W. Law, M.A.* (1892-93). *A Serious Call* is available in editions new and old.

A Practical Treatise on Christian Perfection

CHAPTER II
CHRISTIANITY REQUIRES A CHANGE OF NATURE: A NEW LIFE PERFECTLY DEVOTED TO GOD

Christianity is not a school, for the teaching of moral virtue, the polishing our manners, or forming us to live a life of this world with decency and gentility.

It is deeper and more divine in its designs, and has much nobler ends than these, it implies an entire change of life, a dedication of ourselves, our souls and bodies unto God, in the strictest and highest sense of the words.

Our blessed Saviour came into the world not to make any composition with it, or to divide things between heaven and earth, but to make war with every state of life, to put an end to the designs of flesh and blood, and to show us, that we must either leave this world, to become sons of God, or by enjoying it, take our portion amongst devils and damned spirits.

Death is not more certainly a separation of our souls from our bodies, than the Christian life is a separation of our souls from worldly tempers, vain indulgences, and unnecessary cares.

No sooner are we baptized, but we are to consider ourselves as new and holy persons, that are entered upon a new state of things, that are devoted to God, and have renounced all, to be fellow-heirs with Christ, and members of his kingdom.

There is no alteration of life, no change of condition, that implies half so much, as that alteration which Christianity introduceth.

It is a kingdom of heaven begun upon earth, and by being made members of it, we are entered into a new state of goods and evils.

Eternity altereth the face and nature of everything in this world, life is only a trial, prosperity becometh adversity, pleasure a mischief, and nothing a good, but as it increaseth our hope, purifieth our natures, and prepareth us to receive higher degrees of happiness.

Let us now see what it is, to enter into this state of redemption.

Our own church in conformity with scripture, and the practice of the purest ages, makes it necessary for us to renounce the pomps and vanities of the world, before we can be received as members of Christian communion.

Did we enough consider this, we should find, that whenever we yield ourselves up to the pleasures, profits, and honours of this life, that we turn apostates, break our covenant with God, and go back from the express conditions, on which we were admitted into the communion of Christ's church.

If we consult either the life or doctrines of our Saviour, we shall find that Christianity is a covenant, that contains only the terms of changing and resigning this world, for another, that is to come.

It is a state of things that wholly regards eternity, and knows of no other goods, and evils, but such as relate to another life.

It is a kingdom of heaven, that has no other interests in this world, than as it takes its members out of it, and when the number of the elect is complete, this world will be consumed with fire, as having no other reason of its existence than the furnishing members for that blessed Society which is to last for ever.

I cannot here omit observing the folly and vanity of human wisdom, which full of imaginary projects, pleases itself with its mighty prosperities, its lasting establishments in a world doomed to destruction, and which is to last no longer, than till a sufficient number are redeemed out of it.

Did we see a number of animals hastening to take up their apartments, and contending for the best places, in a building that was to be beat down, as soon as its old inhabitants were got safe out, we should see a contention full as wise, as the wisdom of worldly ambition.

To return. Christianity is therefore a course of holy discipline, solely fitted to the cure and recovery of fallen spirits, and intends such a change in our nature, as may raise us to a nearer union with God, and qualify us for such high degrees of happiness.

It is no wonder therefore, if it makes no provision for the flesh, if it condemns the maxims of human wisdom, and indulges us in no worldly projects, since its very end is to redeem us from all the vanity, vexation, and misery, of this state of things, and to place us in a condition, where we shall be fellow-heirs with Christ, and as the angels of God.

That Christianity requires a change of nature, a new life perfectly devoted to God, is plain from the spirit and tenor of the gospel.

The Saviour of the world saith, that except a man be born again, of the water and the Spirit, he cannot enter into the kingdom of God. We are told, that to as as many as received him, to them he gave power, to become the sons of God, which were born, not of blood, nor of the will of the flesh, nor of the will of man, but of God.

These words plainly teach us, that Christianity implies some great change of nature, that as our birth was to us the beginning of a new life, and brought us into a society of earthly enjoyments, so Christianity is another birth, that brings us into a condition altogether as new, as when we first saw the light.

We begin again to be, we enter upon fresh terms of life, have new relations, new hopes and fears, and an entire change of everything that can be called good or evil.

This new birth, this principle of a new life, is the very essence and soul of Christianity, it is the seal of the promises, the mark of our sonship, the earnest of the inheritance, the security of our hope, and the foundation of all our acceptance with God.

He that is in Christ, saith the apostle, is a new creature, and if any man hath not the Spirit of Christ, he is none of his.

And again, He who is joined to the Lord, is one Spirit.

It is not therefore any number of moral virtues, no partial obedience, no modes of worship, no external acts of adoration, no articles of faith, but a new principle of life, an entire change of temper, that makes us true Christians.

If the Spirit of him who raised up Jesus from the dead dwell in you, he that raised up Christ from the dead, shall also quicken your mortal bodies by his Spirit that dwelleth in you. For as many as are led by the Spirit of God, they are the sons of God.

Since therefore the scriptures thus absolutely require a life suitable to the Spirit and temper of Jesus Christ, since they allow us not the privilege of the sons of God, unless we live and act according to the Spirit of God; it is past doubt, that Christianity requires an entire change of nature and temper, a life devoted perfectly to God.

For what can imply a greater change, than from a carnal to a spiritual mind? What can be more contrary, than the works of the flesh are to the works of the Spirit? It is the difference of heaven and hell.

Light and darkness are but faint resemblances of that great contrariety, that is betwixt the Spirit of God, and the spirit of the world.

Its wisdom is foolishness, its friendship is enmity with God.

All that is in the world, the lust of the flesh, the lust of the eyes, and the pride of life, is not of the Father.

Worldly opinions, proud reasonings, fleshly cares, and earthly projects, are all so many false judgments, mere lies, and we know who is the father of lies.

For this reason, the scripture makes the devil the god and prince of this world, because the spirit and temper which reigns there, is entirely from him; and so far as we are governed by the wisdom and temper of the world, so far are we governed by that evil power of darkness.

If we would see more of this contrariety, and what a change our new life in Christ implies, let us consider what it is to be born of God.

St. John tells us one sure mark of our new birth, in the following words: He that is born of God, overcometh the world.

So that the new birth, or the Christian life, is considered with opposition to the world, and all that is in it, its vain cares, its false glories, proud designs, and sensual pleasures, if we have overcome these, so as to be governed by other cares, other glories, other designs, and other pleasures, then are we born of God. Then is the wisdom of this world, and the friendship of this world, turned into the wisdom and friendship of God, which will for ever keep us heirs of God, and joint-heirs with Christ.

Again, the same apostle helps us to another sign of our new life in God. Whosoever, saith he, is born of God, doth not commit sin, for his seed remaineth in him, and he cannot sin, because he is born of God.

This is not to be understood, as if he that was born of God, was therefore in an absolute state of perfection, and incapable afterwards of falling into anything that was sinful.

It only means, that he that is born of God, is possessed of a temper and principle, that makes him utterly hate and labour to avoid all sin; he is therefore said not to commit sin, in such a sense as a man may be said not to do that, which it is his constant care and principle to prevent being done.

He cannot sin, as it may be said of a man that has no principle but covetousness, that he cannot do things that are expensive, because it is his constant care and labour to be sparing, and if expense happen, it is contrary to his intention; it is his pain and trouble, and he returns to saving with a double diligence.

Thus is he that is born of God, purity and holiness is his only aim, and he is more incapable of having any sinful intentions, than the miser is incapable of generous expense, and if he finds himself in any sin, it is his greatest pain and trouble, and he labours after holiness with a double zeal.

This it is to be born of God, when we have a temper and mind so entirely devoted to purity and holiness, that it may be said of us in a just sense, that we cannot commit sin. When holiness is such a habit in our minds, so directs and forms our designs, as covetousness and ambition directs and governs the actions of such men, as are governed by no other principles, then are we alive in God, and living members of the mystical body of his Son Jesus Christ.

This is our true standard and measure by which we are to judge of ourselves; we are not true Christians unless we are born of God, and we are not born of God, unless it can be said of us in this sense that we cannot commit sin.

When by an inward principle of holiness we stand so disposed to all degrees of virtue, as the ambitious man stands disposed to all steps of greatness, when we hate and avoid all kinds of sins, as the covetous man hates and avoids all sorts of loss and expense, then are we such sons of God, as cannot commit sin.

We must therefore examine into the state and temper of our minds, and see whether we be thus changed in our natures, thus born again to a new life, whether we be so spiritual, as to have overcome the world, so holy, as that we cannot commit sin; since it is the undeniable doctrine of scripture, that this state of mind, this new birth is as necessary to salvation, as the believing in Jesus Christ.

To be eminent therefore for any particular virtue, to detest and avoid several kinds of sins, is just nothing at all; its excellency (as the apostle saith of some particular virtues) is but as sounding brass and a tinkling cymbal.

But when the temper and taste of our soul is entirely changed, when we are renewed in the spirit of our minds, and are full of a relish and desire of all godliness, of a fear and abhorrence of all evil, then, as St. John speaks, may we know that we are of the truth, and shall assure our hearts before him, then shall we know, that he abideth in us by the Spirit, which he hath given us.

We have already seen two marks of those that are born of God: the one is, that they have overcome the world, the other, that they do not commit sin.

To these I shall only add a third, which is given us by Christ himself: I say unto you, love your enemies, bless them that curse you, do good to them that hate you, and pray for them which despitefully use you, and persecute you, that you may be the children of your Father which is in Heaven.

Well may a Christian be said to be a new creature, and Christianity an entire change of temper, since such a disposition as this, is made so necessary, that without it, we cannot be the children of our Father which is in heaven; and if we are not his children, neither is he our Father.

It is not therefore enough, that we love our friends, benefactors, and relations, but we must love like God, if we will show that we are born of him. We must like him have a universal love and tenderness for all mankind, imitating that Love, which would that all men should be saved.

God is love, and this we are to observe, as the true standard of ourselves, that he who dwelleth in God, dwelleth in love;

and consequently he who dwelleth not in love, dwelleth not in God.

It is impossible therefore to be a true Christian, and an enemy at the same time.

Mankind has no enemy but the devil, and they who partake of his malicious and ill-natured spirit.

There is perhaps no duty of religion that is so contrary to flesh and blood as this, but as difficult as it may seem to a worldly mind, it is still necessary, and will easily be performed by such as are in Christ, new creatures.

For take but away earthly goods and evils, and you take away all hatred and malice, for they are the only causes of those base tempers. He therefore that hath overcome the world, hath overcome all the occasions of envy and ill nature; for having put himself in this situation, he can pity, pray for, and forgive all his enemies, who want less forgiveness from him, than he expects from his heavenly Father.

Let us here awhile contemplate the height and depth of Christian holiness, and that god-like spirit which our religion requireth. This duty of universal love and benevolence, even to our bitterest enemies, may serve to convince us, that to be Christians, we must be born again, change our very natures, and have no governing desire of our souls, but that of being made like God.

For we cannot exercise, or delight in this duty, till we rejoice and delight only in increasing our likeness to God.

We may therefore from this, as well as from what has been before observed, be infallibly assured, that Christianity does not consist in any partial amendment of our lives, any particular moral virtues, but in an entire change of our natural temper, a life wholly devoted to God.

To proceed,

This same doctrine is farther taught by our blessed Saviour, when speaking of little children, he saith, Suffer them to come unto me, for of such is the kingdom of God. And again, Whosoever shall not receive the kingdom of God, as a little child, shall in no wise enter therein.

If we are not resolved to deceive ourselves, to have eyes and see not, ears and hear not, we must perceive that these words imply some mighty change in our nature.

For what can make us more contrary to ourselves, than to lay aside all our manly wisdom, our mature judgments, our boasted abilities, and become infants in nature and temper, before we can partake of this heavenly state?

We reckon it change enough, from babes to be men, and surely it must signify as great an alteration, to be reduced from men to a state of infancy.

One peculiar condition of infants is this, that they have everything to learn, they are to be taught by others what they are to hope and fear, and wherein their proper happiness consists.

It is in this sense, that we are chiefly to become as infants, to be as though that we had everything to learn, and suffer ourselves to be taught what we are to choose, and what to avoid; to pretend to no wisdom of our own, but be ready to pursue that happiness which God in Christ proposes to us, and to accept it with such simplicity of mind, as children, that have nothing of our own to oppose to it.

But now, is this infant-temper thus essential to the Christian life? Does the kingdom of God consist only of such as are so affected? Let this then be added as another undeniable proof, that Christianity requires a new nature, and temper of mind; and that this temper is such, as having renounced the prejudices of life, the maxims of human wisdom, yields itself with a child-like submission and simplicity to be entirely governed by the precepts and doctrines of Christ.

Craft and policy, selfish cunning, proud abilities, and vain endowments, have no admittance into this holy state of society with Christ and God.

The wisdom of this world, the intrigues of life, the designs of greatness and ambition, lead to another kingdom, and he that would follow Christ, must empty himself of this vain furniture, and put on the meek ornaments of infant and undesigning simplicity.

Where is the wise? Where is the scribe? Where is the disputer of this world? saith the apostle, Hath not God made foolish the wisdom of this world?

If therefore we will partake of the wisdom of God, we must think and judge of this world, and its most boasted gifts, as the wisdom of God judgeth of them; we must deem them foolishness, and with undivided hearts labour after one wisdom, one perfection, one happiness, in being entirely devoted to God.

This comparison of the spirit of a Christian, to the temper of children, may also serve to recommend to us a certain simplicity of manners, which is a great ornament of behaviour, and is indeed always the effect of a heart entirely devoted to God.

For as the tempers of men are made designing and deceitful, by their having many and secret ends to bring about, so the heart that is entirely devoted to God, is at unity with itself, and all others; it being wholly taken up with one great design, has no little successes that it labours after, and so is naturally open, simple, and undesigning in all the affairs of life.

Although what has been already observed in the foregoing pages might be thought sufficient to show, that Christianity requires a new nature, a life entirely devoted to God; yet since the scriptures add other evidences of the same truth, I must quote a passage or two more on this head.

The Holy Spirit of God is not satisfied with representing that change which Christianity introduceth, by telling us, that it is a new birth, a being born of God, and the like, but proceeds to convince us of the same truth by another way of speaking, by representing it as a state of death.

Thus saith the apostle, ye are dead, and your life is hid with Christ in God.

That is, you Christians are dead as to this world, and the life which you now live, is not to be reckoned by any visible or worldly goods, but is hid in Christ, is a spiritual enjoyment, a life of faith, and not of sight; ye are members of that mystical body of which Christ is the head, and entered into a kingdom which is not of this world

And in this state of death are we as Christians to continue till Christ, who is our life, shall appear, and then shall we also appear with him in glory.

To show us that this death begins with our Christian state, we are said to be buried with him in baptism; so that we entered into this state of death at our baptism, when we entered into Christianity.

Know ye not, says the apostle, that so many of us as were baptized into Jesus Christ, were baptized into his death? Therefore we are buried with him, by baptism into death.

Now Christians may be said to be baptized into the death of Christ, if their baptism puts them into a state like to that, in which our Saviour was at his death. The apostle shows this to be the meaning of it, by saying, if we have been planted together in the likeness of his death, that is, if our baptism has put us into a state like that of his death.

So that Christian baptism is not only an external rite, by which we are entered into the external society of Christ's Church, but is a solemn consecration, which presents us an offering to God, as Christ was offered at his death.

We are therefore no longer alive to the enjoyments of this world, but as Christ was then nailed to the cross, and devoted entirely to God, that he might be made perfect through sufferings, and ascend to the Right Hand of God; so is our old man to be crucified, and we consecrated to God, by a conformity to the death of Christ, that like as Christ was raised from the dead by the glory of the Father, even so we also should walk in newness of life, and being risen with Christ, should seek those things which are above.

This is the true undeniable state of Christianity; baptism does not make us effectually Christians, unless it brings us into a state of death, consecrates us to God, and begins a life suitable to that state of things, to which our Saviour is risen from the dead. This, and no other than this, is the holiness, and spiritual temper, of the Christian life, which implies such a resignation of mind, such a dedication of ourselves to God, as may resemble the death of Christ. And on the other hand, such a newness of life, such an ascension of the soul, such a holy and heavenly behaviour, as may show that we are risen with Christ, and belong to that glorious state, where he now sits at the right hand of God.

It is in this sense, that the holy Jesus saith of his disciples, they are not of this world, even as I am not of this world; being not left to live the life of the world, but chosen out of it for the purposes of his kingdom, that they might copy after his death, and oblation of himself to God.

And this is the condition of all Christians to the consummation of all things, who are to carry on the same designs, and by the same means raise out of this corrupted state, a number of fellow-heirs with Christ in everlasting glory. The Saviour of the world has purchased mankind with his blood, not to live in ease and pleasurable enjoyments, not to spend their time in softness and luxury, in the gratifications of pride, idleness, and vanity, but to drink of his cup, to be baptized with the baptism that he was baptized with, to make war with their corrupt natures, humble themselves, mortify the desires of the flesh, and like him to be made perfect through sufferings.

St. Paul so well knew this to be the design and spirit of religion, that he puts his title to the benefits of Christ's resurrection upon it, when he says,

That I may know him and the power of his resurrection, and the fellowship of his sufferings, being made conformable to his death.

It is his being made conformable to his death, on which he founds his hopes of sharing in the resurrection of Christ. If Christians think that salvation is now to be had on softer terms, and that a life of indulgence and sensual gratifications is consistent with the terms of the gospel, and that they need not now be made conformable to his death, they are miserably blind, and as much mistake their Saviour, as the worldly Jews who expected a temporal Messiah to deliver them.

Our redemption is a redemption by sacrifice, and none are redeemed, but they who conform to it. If we suffer with him we shall also reign with him.

We must then, if we would be wise unto salvation, die and rise again like Christ, and make all the actions of our life holy by offering them to God. Whether we eat, or drink, or whatsoever we do, we must do all to the glory of God.

Since therefore, he that is called to Christianity, is thus called to an imitation of the death of Christ, to forbear from sin, to overcome the world, to be born of the Spirit, to be born of God, these surely will be allowed to be sufficient evidences, that Christianity requireth an entire change of our nature, a life perfectly devoted to God.

Now if this is Christian piety, it may serve to instruct two sorts of people:

First, those who are content with an outward decency and regularity of life: I don't mean such as are hypocritical in their virtues; but all those who are content with an outward form of behaviour, without that inward newness of heart and spirit which the Gospel requireth.

Charity, chastity, sobriety, and justice, may be practised without Christian piety: a Jew, a heathen, may be charitable and temperate; but to make these virtues become parts of Christian piety, they must proceed from a heart truly turned unto God, that is full of an infant simplicity, that is crucified with Christ, that is born again of the Spirit, that has overcome the world. Temperance or justice without this turn of heart, may be the temperance of a Jew or a heathen, but it is not Christian temperance till it proceed from a true Christian spirit. Could we do and suffer all that Christ himself did or suffered, yet if it was not all done in the same spirit and temper of Christ, we should have none of his merit.

A Christian therefore must be sober, charitable, and just, upon the same principles, and with the same spirit, that he receives the holy sacrament, for ends of religion, as acts of obedience to God, as means of purity and holiness, and as so many instances of a heart devoted to God.

As the bare eating of bread, and drinking wine in the holy sacrament, is of no use to us, without those religious dispositions which constitute the true frame of a pious mind, so is it the same in all other duties; they are mere outward ceremonies, and useless actions, unless they are performed in the spirit of religion: charity and sobriety are of no value, till they are so many instances of a heart truly devoted to God.

A Christian therefore is to be sober, not only so far as answers the ends of a decent and orderly life, but in such a manner as becomes one, who is born of the Holy Spirit, that is made one with Christ, who dwells in Christ and Christ in him. He must be sober in such a measure as best serves the ends of religion, and practise such abstinence as may make him fittest for the holiness, purity, and perfection of the Christian life.

He must be charitable, not so far as suits with humanity and good esteem amongst men, but in such a measure as is according to the doctrines and spirit of religion.

For neither charity, nor temperance, nor any other virtue, are parts of Christian holiness, till they are made holy and religious by such a piety of heart, as shows that we live wholly unto God.

This is what cannot be too much considered by a great many people, whose religion has made no change in their hearts, but only consists in an external decency of life, who are sober without the piety of sobriety, who pray without devotion, who give alms without charity, and are Christians without the spirit of Christianity.

Let them remember that religion is to alter our nature, that Christian piety consists in a change of heart, that it implies a new turn of spirit, a spiritual death, a spiritual life, a dying to the world, and a living wholly unto God.

Secondly, this doctrine may serve to instruct those who have lived strangers to religion, what they are to do to become true Christians.

Some people who are ashamed of the folly of their lives, and begin to look towards religion, think they have done enough, when they either alter the outward course of their lives, abate some of the extravagances, or become careful of some particular virtue.

Thus a man, whose life has been a course of folly, thinks he has made a sufficient change, by becoming temperate. Another imagines he has sufficiently declared for religion, by not neglecting the public worship as he used to do. A lady fancies that she lives enough to God, because she has left off plays and paint, and lives more at home, than in the former part of her life.

But such people should consider, that religion is no one particular virtue; that it does not consist in the fewness of our vices, or in any particular amendment of our lives, but in such a thorough change of heart, as makes piety and holiness the measure and rule of all our tempers.

It is a miserable error to be content with ourselves, because we are less vain, or covetous, more sober, and decent in our behaviour, than we used to be; yet this is the state of many people, who think they have sufficiently reformed their lives, because they are in some degree different from what they were. They think it enough to be changed from what they were, without considering how thorough a change religion requires.

But let such people remember, that they who thus measure themselves by themselves are not wise. Let them remember that they are not disciples of Christ, till they have like him offered their whole body and soul as a reasonable and lively sacrifice unto God; that they are not members of Christ's mystical body, till they are united unto him by a new spirit; that they have not entered into the kingdom of God, till they have entered with an infant simplicity of heart, till they are so born again as not to commit sin, so full of an heavenly spirit, as to have overcome the world.

Nothing less than this great change of heart and mind can give anyone any assurance, that he is truly turned to God. There is but this one term of salvation, He that is in Christ, is a new creature. How insignificant all other attainments are, is sufficiently shown in the following words: Many will say to me in that day, Lord, Lord, have we not prophesied in thy name? And in thy name have cast out devils? And in thy name have done many wonderful works? And then will I profess unto them, I never knew you. Depart from me, ye that work iniquity.

So that there is no religion that will stand us in any stead, but that which is the conversion of the heart to God; when all our tempers are tempers of piety, springing from a soul that is born again of the Spirit, that tends with one full bent to a perfection and happiness in the enjoyment of God.

Let us therefore look carefully to ourselves, and consider what manner of spirit we are of; let us not think our condition safe, because we are of this or that church or communion, or because we are strict observers of the external offices of religion, for these are marks that belong to more than belong to Christ. All are not his, that prophesy or even work miracles in his name, much less those, who with worldly minds and corrupt hearts are only baptized in his name.

If religion has raised us into a new world, if it has filled us with new ends of life, if it has taken possession of our hearts, and altered the whole turn of our minds, if it has changed all our ideas of things, given us a new set of hopes and fears, and taught us to live by the realities of an invisible world, then may we humbly hope, that we are true followers of the holy Jesus, and such as may rejoice in the day of Christ, that we have neither run in vain, nor laboured in vain.

A Serious Call to a Devout and Holy Life

CHAPTER I
CONCERNING THE NATURE AND EXTENT OF
CHRISTIAN DEVOTION

Devotion is neither private nor public prayer, but prayers whether private or public, are particular parts or instances of devotion. Devotion signifies a life given, or devoted to God.

He therefore is the devout man, who lives no longer to his own will, or the way and spirit of the world, but to the sole will of God, who considers God in everything, who serves God in everything, who makes all the parts of his common life, parts of piety, by doing everything in the name of God, and under such rules as are conformable to his glory.

We readily acknowledge that God alone is to be the rule and measure of our prayers; that in them we are to look wholly unto him, and act wholly for him; that we are only to pray in such a manner, for such things, and such ends, as are suitable to his glory.

Now let anyone but find out the reason, why he is to be thus strictly pious in his prayers, and he will find the same as strong a reason, to be as strictly pious in all the other parts of his life. For there is not the least shadow of a reason, why we should make God the rule and measure of our prayers; why we should then look wholly unto him, and pray according to his will; but what equally proves it necessary for us to look wholly unto God, and make him the rule and measure of all the other actions of our life. For any ways of life, any employment of our talents, whether of our parts, our time, or money, that is not strictly according to the will of God, that is not for such ends as are suitable to his glory, are as great absurdities and failings, as prayers that are not according to the will of God. For there is no other reason, why our prayers should be according to the will of God, why they should have nothing in them, but what is wise, and holy, and heavenly, there is no other reason for this, but that our lives may be of the same nature, full of the same wisdom, holiness, and heavenly tempers, that we may live unto God in the same spirit that we pray unto him. Were it not our strict duty to live by reason, to devote all the actions of our lives to God, were it not absolutely necessary to walk before him in wisdom and holiness and all heavenly conversation, doing everything in his name, and for his glory, there would be no excellency or wisdom in the most heavenly prayers. Nay, such prayers would be absurdities, they would be like prayers for wings, when it was no part of our duty to fly.

As sure, therefore, as there is any wisdom in praying for the spirit of God, so sure is it, that we are to make that spirit the rule of all our actions; as sure as it is our duty to look wholly unto God in our prayers, so sure is it, that it is our duty to live wholly unto God in our lives. But we can no more be said to live unto God, unless we live unto him in all the ordinary actions of our life, unless he be the rule and measure of all our ways, than we can be said to pray unto God, unless our prayers look wholly unto him. So that unreasonable and absurd ways of life, whether in labour or diversion, whether they consume our time, or our money, are like unreasonable and absurd prayers, and are as truly an offence unto God.

'Tis for want of knowing, or at least considering this, that we see such a mixture of ridicule in the lives of so many people. You see them strict as to some times and places of devotion, but when the service of the church is over, they are but like those who seldom or never come there. In their way of life, their manner of spending their time and money, in their cares and fears, in their pleasures and indulgences, in their labour and diversions, they are like the rest of the world. This makes the loose part of the world generally make a jest of those who are devout, because they see their devotion goes no further than their prayers, and that when they are over, they live no more unto God, till the time of prayer returns again; but live by the same humour and fancy, and in as full an enjoyment of all the follies of life as other people. This is the reason why they are the jest and scorn of careless and worldly people; not because they are really devoted to God, but because they appear to have no other devotion, but that of occasional prayers.

Julius is very fearful of missing prayers; all the parish supposes Julius to be sick, if he is not at church. But if you were to ask him why he spends the rest of his time by humour and chance? why he is a companion of the silliest people in their most silly pleasures? why he is ready for every impertinent entertainment and diversion? If you were to ask him why there is no amusement too trifling to please him? why he is busy at all balls and assemblies? why he gives himself up to an idle gossiping conversation? why he lives in foolish friendships and fondness of particular persons, that neither want not deserve any particular kindness? why he allows himself in foolish hatreds and resentments against particular persons, without considering that he is to love everybody as himself? If you ask him why he never puts his conversation, his time, and fortune, under the rules of religion, Julius has no more to say for himself, than the most disorderly person. For the whole tenor of scripture lies as directly against such a life, as against debauchery and intemperance: he that lives in such a course of idleness and folly, lives no more according to the religion of Jesus Christ, than he that lives in gluttony and intemperance.

If a man were to tell Julius that there was no occasion for so much constancy at prayers, and that he might, without any harm to himself, neglect the service of the church, as the generality of people do, Julius would think such a one to be no Christian, and that he ought to avoid his company. But if a person only tells him, that he may live as the generality of the world does, that he may enjoy himself as others do, that he may spend his time and money as people of fashion do, that he may conform to the follies and frailties of the generality, and gratify his tempers and passions as most people do, Julius never suspects that man to want a Christian spirit, or that he is doing the devil's work.

And if Julius were to read all the New Testament from the beginning to the end, he would find his course of life condemned in every page of it.

And indeed there cannot anything be imagined more absurd

in itself, than wise and sublime, and heavenly prayers, added to a life of vanity and folly, where neither labour nor diversions, neither time nor money, are under the direction of the wisdom and heavenly tempers of our prayers. If we were to see a man pretending to act wholly with regard to God in everything that he did, that would neither spend time or money, or take any labour or diversion, but so far as he could act according to strict principles of reason and piety, and yet at the same time neglect all prayer, whether public or private, should we not be amazed at such a man, and wonder how he could have so much folly along with so much religion?

Yet this is as reasonable, as for any person to pretend to strictness in devotion, to be careful of observing times and places of prayer, and yet letting the rest of his life, his time, and labour, his talents and money, be disposed of without any regard to strict rules of piety and devotion. For it is as great an absurdity to suppose holy prayers and divine petitions without an holiness of life suitable to them, as to suppose an holy and divine life without prayers.

Let anyone therefore think, how easily he could confute a man that pretended to great strictness of life without prayer, and the same arguments will as plainly confute another, that pretends to strictness of prayer, without carrying the same strictness into every other part of life. For to be weak and foolish in spending our time and fortune, is no greater a mistake, than to be weak and foolish in relation to our prayers. And to allow ourselves in any ways of life that neither are, nor can be offered to God, is the same irreligion, as to neglect our prayers, or use them in such a manner, as makes them an offering unworthy of God.

The short of the matter is this, either reason and religion prescribe rules and ends to all the ordinary actions of our life, or they do not: if they do, then it is as necessary to govern all our actions by those rules, as it is necessary to worship God. For if religion teaches us anything concerning eating and drinking, or spending our time and money; if it teaches us how we are to use and contemn the world; if it tells us what tempers we are to have in common life, how we are to be disposed towards all people, how we are to behave towards the sick, the poor, the old and destitute; if it tells us whom we are to treat with a particular love, whom we are to regard with a particular esteem; if it tells us how we are to treat our enemies, and how we are to mortify and deny ourselves, he must be very weak, that can think these parts of religion are not to be observed with as much exactness as any doctrines that relate to prayers.

It is very observable, that there is not one command in all the gospel for public worship; and perhaps it is a duty that is least insisted upon in scripture of any other. The frequent attendance at it is never so much as mentioned in all the New Testament. Whereas that religion or devotion which is to govern the ordinary actions of our life, is to be found in almost every verse of Scripture. Our blessed Saviour and his apostles are wholly taken up in doctrines that relate to common life. They call us to renounce the world, and differ in every temper and way of life, from the spirit and way of the world: to renounce all its goods, to fear none of its evils, to reject its joys, and have no value for its happiness: to be as new born babies, that are born into a new state of things; to live as pilgrims in spiritual watching, in holy fear, and heavenly aspiring after another life: to take up our daily cross, to deny ourselves, to profess the blessedness of mourning, to seek the blessedness of poverty of spirit: to forsake the pride and vanity of riches, to take no thought for the morrow, to live in the profoundest state of humility, to rejoice in worldly sufferings: to reject the lust of the flesh, the lust of the eyes, and the pride of life; to bear injuries, to forgive and bless our enemies, and to love mankind as God loveth them: to give up our whole hearts and affections to God, and strive to enter through the strait gate into a life of eternal glory.

This is the common devotion which our blessed Saviour taught, in order to make it the common life of all Christians. Is it not therefore exceeding strange, that people should place so much piety in the attendance upon public worship, concerning which there is not one precept of our Lord's to be found, and yet neglect these common duties of our ordinary life, which are commanded in every page of the gospel? I call these duties the devotion of our common life, because if they are to be practised, they must be made parts of our common life, they can have no place anywhere else.

If contempt of the world and heavenly affection, is a necessary temper of Christians, it is necessary that this temper appear in the whole course of their lives, in their manner of using the world, because it can have no place anywhere else.

If self-denial be a condition of salvation, all that would be saved, must make it a part of their ordinary life. If humility be a Christian duty, then the common life of a Christian, is to be a constant course of humility in all its kinds. If poverty of spirit be necessary, it must be the spirit and temper of every day of our lives. If we are to relieve the naked, the sick, and the prisoner, it must be the common charity of our lives, as far as we can render ourselves able to perform it. If we are to love our enemies, we must make our common life a visible exercise and demonstration of that love. If content and thankfulness, if the patient bearing of evil be duties to God, they are the duties of every day, and in every circumstance of our life. If we are to be wise and holy as the new-born sons of God, we can no otherwise be so, but by renouncing everything that is foolish and in vain in every part of our common life. If we are to be in Christ new creatures, we must show that we are so, by having new ways of living in the world. If we are to follow Christ, it must be in our common way of spending every day.

Thus it is in all the virtues and holy tempers of Christianity; they are not ours unless they be the virtues and tempers of our ordinary life. So that Christianity is so far from leaving us to live in the common ways of life, conforming to the folly of customs, and gratifying the passions and tempers which the spirit of the world delights in, it is so far from indulging us in any of these things, that all its virtues which it makes necessary to salvation, are only so many ways of living above, and contrary to the world in all the common actions of our life. If our common life is not a common course of humility, self-denial, renunciation of the world, poverty of spirit, and heavenly affection, we do not live the lives of Christians.

But yet though it is thus plain, that this, and this alone is Christianity, an uniform open and visible practice of all these virtues, yet it is as plain, that there is little or nothing of this to be found, even amongst the better sort of people. You see them often at church and pleased with fine preachers, but look into their lives, and you see them just the same sort of people as others are, that make no pretences to devotion. The difference that you find betwixt them, is only the difference of their natural tempers. They have the same taste of the world, the same worldly cares, and fears, and joys; they have the same turn of mind, equally vain in their desires. You see the same fondness for state and equipage, the same pride and vanity of dress, the same self-love and indulgence, the same foolish friendships, and groundless hatreds, the same levity of mind, and trifling spirit, the same fondness for diversions, the same idle dispositions, and vain ways of spending their time in visiting and conversation, as the rest of the world, that make no pretences to devotion.

I do not mean this comparison betwixt people seemingly good, and professed rakes, but betwixt people of sober lives. Let us take an instance in two modest women: let it be supposed, that one of them is careful of times of devotion, and observes them through a sense of duty, and that the other has no hearty concern about it, but is at church seldom or often, just as it happens. Now it is a very easy thing to see this difference betwixt these persons. But when you have seen this, can you find any further difference betwixt them? Can you find that their common life is of a different kind? Are not the tempers, and customs, and manners of the one, of the same kind as of the other? Do they live as if they belonged to different worlds, had different views in their heads, and different rules and measures of all their actions? Have they not the same goods and evils, are they not pleased and displeased in the same manner, and for the same things? Do they not live in the same course of life? Does one seem to be of this world, looking at the things that are temporal, and the other to be of another world, looking wholly at the things that are eternal? Does the one live in pleasure, delighting herself in show or dress, and the other live in self-denial and mortification, renouncing everything that looks like vanity, either of person, dress, or carriage? Does the one follow public diversions, and trifle away her time in idle visits, and corrupt conversation, and does the other study all the arts of improving her time, living in prayer and watching, and such good works as may make all her time turn to her advantage, and be placed to her account at the last day? Is the one careless of expense, and glad to be able to adorn herself with every costly ornament of dress, and does the other consider her fortune as a talent given her by God, which is to be improved religiously, and no more to be spent in vain and needless ornaments, than it is to be buried in the earth?

Where must you look, to find one person of religion differing in this manner, from another that has none? And yet if they do not differ in these things which are here related, can it with any sense be said, the one is a good Christian, and the other not?

Take another instance amongst the men. Leo has a great deal of good nature, has kept what they call good company, hates everything that is false and base, is very generous and brave to his friends, but has concerned himself so little with religion, that he hardly knows the difference betwixt a Jew and a Christian.

Eusebius on the other hand, has had early impressions of religion, and buys books of devotion. He can talk of all the feasts and fasts of the church, and knows the names of most men that have been eminent for piety. You never hear him swear, or make a loose jest, and when he talks of religion, he talks of it, as of a matter of the last concern.

Here you see, that one person has religion enough, according to the way of the world, to be reckoned a pious Christian, and the other is so far from all appearance of religion, that he may fairly be reckoned a heathen; and yet if you look into their common life, if you examine their chief and ruling tempers in the greatest articles of life, or the greatest doctrines of Christianity, you will find the least difference imaginable.

Consider them with regard to the use of the world, because that is what everybody can see.

Now to have right notions and tempers with relation to this world, is as essential to religion, as to have right notions of God.

And it is as possible for a man to worship a crocodile, and yet be a pious man, as to have his affections set upon this world, and yet be a good Christian.

But now if you consider Leo and Eusebius in this respect, you will find them exactly alike, seeking, using, and enjoying all that can be got in this world in the same manner, and for the same ends. You will find that riches, prosperity, pleasures, indulgences, state, and honour, are just as much the happiness of Eusebius as they are of Leo. And yet if Christianity has not changed a man's mind and temper with relation to these things, what can we say that it has done for him?

For if the doctrines of Christianity were practised, they would make a man as different from other people as to all worldly tempers, sensual pleasures, and the pride of life, as a wise man is different from a natural; it would be as easy a thing to know a Christian by his outward course of life, as it is now difficult to find anybody that lives it. For it is notorious, that Christians are now not only like other men in their frailties and infirmities, this might be in some degree excusable, but the complaint is, they are like heathens in all the main and chief articles of their lives. They enjoy the world, and live every day in the same tempers, and the same designs, and the same indulgences, as they do who know not God, nor of any happiness in another life. Everybody who is capable of any reflection, must have observed, that this is generally the state even of devout people, whether men or women. You may see them different from other people, so far as to times and places of prayer, but generally like the rest of the world in all the other parts of their lives. That is, adding Christian devotion to a heathen life: I have the authority of our blessed Saviour for his remark, where he says, 'Take no thought, saying what shall we eat, or what shall we drink, or wherewithal shall we be clothed? for after all these things do the Gentiles seek.' But if to be thus affected, even with the necessary things of this life, shows that we are not yet of a Christian spirit, but are like the heathens, surely to enjoy the vanity and folly of the world as they did, to be like them in the main chief tempers of our lives, in self-love and indulgence, in sensual pleasures and diversions, in the vanity of dress, the love of show and greatness, or any other gaudy distinctions of fortune, is a much greater sign of a heathen temper. And consequently, they who add devotion to such a life, must be said to pray as Christians, but live as heathens.

CHAPTER VII
HOW THE IMPRUDENT USE OF AN ESTATE CORRUPTS ALL THE TEMPERS OF THE MIND, AND FILLS THE HEART WITH POOR AND RIDICULOUS PASSIONS, THROUGH THE WHOLE COURSE OF LIFE; REPRESENTED IN THE CHARACTER OF FLAVIA

It has already been observed, that a prudent and religious care is to be used, in the manner of spending our money or estate, because the manner of spending our estates makes so great a part of our common life, and is so much the business of every day, that according as we are wise, or imprudent, in this respect, the whole course of our lives, will be rendered either very wise, or very full of folly.

Persons that are well affected to religion, that receive instructions of piety with pleasure and satisfaction, often wonder how it comes to pass, that they make no greater progress in that religion which they so much admire.

Now the reason of it is this; it is because religion lives only in their head, but something else has possession of their hearts; and therefore they continue from year to year mere admirers, and praisers of piety, without ever coming up to the reality and perfection of its precepts.

If it be asked, why religion does not get possession of their hearts, the reason is this. It is not because they live in gross sins, or debaucheries, for their regard to religion preserves them from such disorders.

But it is because their hearts are constantly employed, perverted, and kept in a wrong state, by the indiscreet use of such things as are lawful to be used.

The use and enjoyment of their estates is lawful, and therefore it never comes into their heads, to imagine any great danger from that quarter. They never reflect, that there is a vain, and imprudent use of their estates, which, though it does not destroy like gross sins, yet so disorders the heart, and supports it in such sensuality and dulness, such pride and vanity, as makes it incapable of receiving the life and spirit of piety.

For our souls may receive an infinite hurt, and be rendered incapable of all virtues, merely by the use of innocent and lawful things.

What is more innocent than rest and retirement? And yet what more dangerous, than sloth and idleness? What is more lawful than eating and drinking? And yet what more destructive of all virtue, what more fruitful of all vice, than sensuality and indulgence?

How lawful and praiseworthy is the care of a family? And yet how certainly are many people rendered incapable of all virtue, by a worldly and solicitous temper?

Now it is for want of religious exactness in the use of these innocent and lawful things, that religion cannot get possession of our hearts. And it is in the right and prudent management of ourselves, as to these things, that all the arts of holy living chiefly consist.

Gross sins are plainly seen, and easily avoided by persons that profess religion. But the indiscreet and dangerous use of innocent and lawful things, as it does not shock and offend our consciences, so it is difficult to make people at all sensible of the danger of it.

A gentleman that expends all his estate in sports, and a woman that lays out all her fortune upon herself, can hardly be persuaded that the spirit of religion cannot subsist in such a way of life.

These persons, as has been observed, may live free from debaucheries, they may be friends of religion, so far as to praise and speak well of it, and admire it in their imaginations; but it cannot govern their hearts, and be the spirit of their actions, till they change their way of life, and let religion give laws to the use and spending of their estates.

For a woman that loves dress, that thinks no expense too great to bestow upon the adorning of her person, cannot stop there. For that temper draws a thousand other follies along with it, and will render the whole course of her life, her business, her conversation, her hopes, her fears, her tastes, her pleasures, and diversions, all suitable to it.

Flavia and Miranda are two maiden sisters, that have each of them two hundred pounds a year. They buried their parents, twenty years ago, and have since that time spent their estate as they pleased.

Flavia has been the wonder of all her friends, for her excellent management, in making so surprising a figure in so moderate a fortune. Several ladies that have twice her fortune, are not able to be always so genteel, and so constant at all places of pleasure and expense. She has everything that is in the fashion, and is in every place where there is any diversion. Flavia is very orthodox, she talks warmly against heretics and schismatics, is generally at church, and often at the sacrament. She once commended a sermon that was against the pride and vanity of dress, and thought it was very just against Lucinda, whom she takes to be a great deal finer than she need be. If anyone asks Flavia to do something in charity, if she likes the person who makes the proposal, or happens to be in a right temper, she will toss him half-a-crown or a crown, and tell him, if he knew what a long milliner's bill she had just received, he would think it a great deal for her to give. A quarter of a year after this, she hears a sermon upon the necessity of charity; she thinks the man preaches well, that it is a very proper subject, that people want much to be put in mind of it; but she applies nothing to herself, because she remembers that she gave a crown some time ago, when she could so ill spare it.

As for poor people themselves, she will admit of no complaints from them; she is very positive they are all cheats and liars; and will say anything to get relief, and therefore it must be a sin to encourage them in their evil ways.

You would think Flavia had the tenderest conscience in the world; if you were to see, how scrupulous and apprehensive she is of the guilt and danger of giving amiss.

She buys all books of wit and humour, and has made an expensive collection of all our English poets. For she says, one cannot have a true taste of any of them, without being very conversant with them all. She will sometimes read a book of piety, if it is a short one, if it is much commended for style and language, and she can tell where to borrow it.

Flavia is very idle, and yet very fond of fine work; this makes her often sit working in bed until noon, and be told many a long story before she is up; so that I need not tell you, that her morning devotions are not always rightly performed.

Flavia would be a miracle of piety, if she were but half so careful of her soul, as she is of her body. The rising of a pimple in her face, the sting of a gnat, will make her keep her room two or three days, and she thinks they are very rash people that do not take care of things in time. This makes her so over-careful of her health, that she never thinks she is well enough; and so over-indulgent, that she never can be really well. So that it costs her a great deal in sleeping-draughts and waking-draughts, in spirits for the head, in drops for the nerves, in cordials for the stomach, and in saffron for her tea.

If you visit Flavia on the Sunday, you will always meet good company, you will know what is doing in the world, you will hear the last lampoon, be told who wrote it, and who is meant by every name that is in it. You will hear what plays were acted that week, which is the finest song in the opera, who was intolerable at the last assembly, and what games are most in fashion. Flavia thinks they are atheists that play at cards on the Sunday, but she will tell you the nicety of all the games, what cards she held, how she played them, and the history of all that happened at play, as soon as she comes from church. If you would know who is rude and ill-natured, who is vain and foppish, who lives too high, and who is in debt: if you would know what is the quarrel at a certain house, or who and who are in love: if you would know how late Belinda comes home at night, what clothes she has bought, how she loves compliments, and what a long story she told at such a place: if you would know how cross Lucius is to his wife, what ill-natured things he says to her, when nobody hears him; if you would know how they hate one another in their hearts, though they appear so kind in public; you must visit Flavia on the Sunday. But still she has so great a regard for the holiness of the Sunday, that she has turned a poor old widow out of her house, as a profane wretch, for having been found once mending her clothes on the Sunday night.

Thus lives Flavia; and if she lives ten years longer, she will have spent about fifteen hundred and sixty Sundays after this manner. She will have worn about two hundred different suits of clothes. Out of this thirty years of her life, fifteen of them will have been disposed of in bed; and of the remaining fifteen, about fourteen of them will have been consumed in eating, drinking, dressing, visiting, conversation, reading and hearing plays and romances, at operas, assemblies, balls and diversions. For you may reckon all the time that she is up, thus spent, except about an hour and half, that is disposed of at church, most Sundays in the year. With great management, and under mighty rules of economy, she will have spent sixty hundred pounds upon herself, bating only some shillings, crowns, or half-crowns, that have gone from her in accidental charities.

I shall not take upon me to say, that it is impossible for Flavia to be saved; but this much must be said, that she has no grounds from scripture to think she is in the way of salvation. For her whole life is in direct opposition to all those tempers and practices, which the gospel has made necessary to salvation.

If you were to hear her say, that she had lived all her life like Anna the prophetess, who departed not from the temple, but served God with fastings and prayers, night and day, you would look upon her as very extravagant; and yet this would be no greater an extravagance, than for her to say, that she has been striving to enter in at the strait gate, or making any one doctrine of the gospel, a rule of her life.

She may as well say, that she lived with our Saviour when he was upon earth, as that she has lived in imitation of him, or made it any part of her care to live in such tempers, as he required of all those that would be his disciples. She may as truly say, that she has every day washed the saints' feet, as that she has lived in Christian humility and poverty of spirit; and as reasonably think, that she has taught a charity-school, as that she has lived in works of charity. She has as much reason to think, that she has been a sentinel in an army, as that she has lived in watching, and self-denial. And it may as fairly be said, that she lived by the labour of her hands, as that she had given all diligence to make her calling and election sure.

And here it is to be well observed, that the poor, vain turn of mind, the irreligion, the folly and vanity of this whole life of Flavia, is all owing to the manner of using her estate. It is this that has formed her spirit, that has given life to every idle temper, that has supported every trifling passion, and kept her from all thoughts of a prudent, useful, and devout life.

When her parents died, she had no thought about her two hundred pounds a year, but that she had so much money to do what she would with, to spend upon herself, and purchase the pleasures and gratifications of all her passions.

And it is this setting out, this false judgment and indiscreet use of her fortune, that has filled her whole life with the same indiscretion, and kept her from thinking of what is right, and wise, and pious in everything else.

If you have seen her delighted in plays and romances, in scandal and backbiting, easily flattered, and soon affronted: if you have seen her devoted to pleasures and diversions, a slave to every passion in its turn, nice in everything that concerned her body or dress, careless of everything that might benefit her soul, always wanting some new entertainment, and ready for every happy invention, in show or dress, it was because she had purchased all these tempers with the yearly revenue of her fortune.

She might have been humble, serious, devout, a lover of good books, an admirer of prayer and retirement, careful of her time, diligent in good works, full of charity and the love of God, but that the imprudent use of her estate forced all the contrary tempers upon her.

And it was no wonder, that she should turn her time, her mind, her health, her strength, to the same uses that she turned her fortune. It is owing to her being wrong in so great an article of life, that you can see nothing wise, or reasonable, or pious in any other part of it.

Now though the irregular trifling spirit of this character belongs, I hope, but to few people, yet many may here learn some instruction from it, and perhaps see something of their own spirit in it.

For as Flavia seems to be undone by the unreasonable use of her fortune, so the lowness of most people's virtue, the imperfections of their piety, and the disorders of their passions, is generally owing to their imprudent use and enjoyment of lawful and innocent things.

More people are kept from a true sense and taste of religion, by a regular kind of sensuality and indulgence, than by gross drunkenness. More men live regardless of the great duties of piety, through too great a concern for worldly goods, than through direct injustice.

This man would perhaps be devout, if he were not so great a virtuoso. Another is deaf to all motives to piety, by indulging an idle, slothful temper.

Could you cure this man of his great curiosity and inquisitive temper, or that of his false satisfaction and thirst after learning, you need do no more to make them both become men of great piety.

If this woman would make fewer visits, or that not be always talking, they would neither of them find it half so hard to be affected with religion.

For all these things are only little, when they are compared to great sins; and though they are little in that respect, yet they are great, as they are impediments and hindrances of a pious spirit.

For as consideration is the only eye of the soul, as the truths of religion can be seen by nothing else, so whatever raises a levity of mind, a trifling spirit, renders the soul incapable of seeing, apprehending, and relishing the doctrines of piety.

Would we therefore make a real progress in religion, we must not only abhor gross and notorious sins, but we must regulate the innocent and lawful parts of our behaviour, and put the most common and allowed actions of life, under the rules of discretion and piety.

CHAPTER VIII
HOW THE WISE AND PIOUS USE OF AN ESTATE, NATURALLY CARRIETH US TO GREAT PERFECTION IN ALL THE VIRTUES OF THE CHRISTIAN LIFE; REPRESENTED IN THE CHARACTER OF MIRANDA

Any one pious regularity of any one part of our life, is of great advantage, not only on its own account, but as it uses us to live by rule, and think of the government of ourselves.

A man of business, that has brought one part of his affairs under certain rules, is in a fair way to take the same care of the rest.

So he that has brought any one part of his life under the rules of religion, may thence be taught to extend the same order and regularity into other parts of his life.

If anyone is so wise as to think his time too precious to be disposed of by chance, and left to be devoured by anything that happens in his way: if he lays himself under a necessity of observing how every day goes through his hands, and obliges himself to a certain order of time in his business, his retirements, and devotions, it is hardly to be imagined, how soon such a conduct would reform, improve, and perfect the whole course of his life.

He that once thus knows the value, and reaps the advantage of a well-ordered time, will not long be a stranger to the value of anything else that is of any real concern to him.

A rule that relates even to the smallest part of our life, is of great benefit to us, merely as it is a rule.

For as the proverb saith, He that has begun well, has half done: So he that has begun to live by rule, has gone a great way towards the perfection of his life.

By rule, must here be constantly understood, a religious rule, observed upon a principle of duty to God.

For if a man should oblige himself to be moderate in his meals, only in regard to his stomach; or abstain from drinking, only to avoid the headache; or be moderate in his sleep, through fear of a lethargy, he might be exact in these rules, without being at all the better man for them.

But when he is moderate and regular in any of these things,

out of a sense of Christian sobriety and self-denial, that he may offer unto God a more reasonable and holy life, then it is, that the smallest rule of this kind, is naturally the beginning of great piety.

For the smallest rule in these matters is of great benefit, as it teaches us some part of the government of ourselves, as it keeps up a tenderness of mind, as it presents God often to our thoughts, and brings a sense of religion into the ordinary actions of our common life.

If a man, whenever he was in company, where anyone swore, talked lewdly, or spoke evil of his neighbour, should make it a rule to himself, either gently to reprove him, or if that was not proper, then to leave the company as decently as he could; he would find, that this little rule, like a little leaven hid in a great quantity of meal, would spread and extend itself through the whole form of his life.

If another should oblige himself to abstain on the Lord's Day from many innocent and lawful things, as travelling, visiting, common conversation, and discoursing upon worldly matters, as trade, news, and the like; if he should devote the day, besides the public worship, to greater retirement, reading, devotion, instruction, and works of charity: though it may seem but a small thing, or a needless nicety, to require a man to abstain from such things as may be done without sin, yet whoever would try the benefit of so little a rule, would perhaps thereby find such a change made in his spirit, and such a taste of piety raised in his mind, as he was an entire stranger to before.

It would be easy to show, in many other instances, how little and small matters are the first steps, and natural beginnings of great perfection.

But the two things which of all others, most want to be under a strict rule, and which are the greatest blessings both to ourselves and others, when they are rightly used, are our time, and our money. These talents are continual means and opportunities of doing good.

He that is piously strict, and exact in the wise management of either of these, cannot be long ignorant of the right use of the other. And he that is happy in the religious care and disposal of them both, has already ascended several steps upon the ladder of Christian perfection.

Miranda (the sister of Flavia) is a sober, reasonable Christian; as soon as she was mistress of her time and fortune, it was her first thought, how she might best fulfil everything that God required of her in the use of them, and how she might make the best and happiest use of this short life. She depends upon the truth of what our blessed Lord hath said, that there is but one thing needful, and therefore makes her whole life but one continual labour after it. She has but one reason for doing, or not doing, for liking, or not liking anything, and that is, the will of God. She is not so weak as to pretend to add, what is called the fine lady, to the true Christian; Miranda thinks too well, to be taken with the sound of such silly words; she has renounced the world to follow Christ in the exercise of humility, charity, devotion, abstinence, and heavenly affections; and that is Miranda's fine breeding.

Whilst she was under her mother, she was forced to be genteel, to live in ceremony, to sit up late at nights, to be in the folly of every fashion, and always visiting on Sundays; to go patched, and loaded with a burden of finery, to the holy sacrament; to be in every polite conversation; to hear profaneness at the playhouse, and wanton songs and love intrigues at the opera; to dance at public places, that fops and rakes might admire the fineness of her shape, and the beauty of her motions. The remembrance of this way of life, makes her exceeding careful to atone for it, by a contrary behaviour.

Miranda does not divide her duty between God, her neighbour, and herself; but she considers all as due to God, and so does everything in his name, and for his sake. This makes her consider her fortune, as the gift of God, that is to be used as everything is, that belongs to God, for the wise and reasonable ends of a Christian and holy life. Her fortune therefore is divided betwixt herself, and several other poor people, and she has only her part of relief from it. She thinks it the same folly to indulge herself in needless, vain expenses, as to give to other people to spend in the same way. Therefore she will not give a poor man money to go see a puppet-show, neither will she allow herself any to spend in the same manner; thinking it very proper to be as wise herself, as she expects poor men should be. For is it a folly and a crime in a poor man, says Miranda, to waste what is given him in foolish trifles, whilst he wants meat, drink, and clothes? And is it less folly, or a less crime in me, to spend that money in silly diversions, which might be so much better spent in imitation of the divine goodness, in works of kindness and charity towards my fellow-creatures, and fellow-Christians? If a poor man's own necessities are a reason why he should not waste any of his money idly, surely the necessities of the poor, the excellency of charity, which is received as done to Christ himself, is a much greater reason why no one should ever waste any of his money. For if he does so, he does not only do like the poor man, only waste that which he wants himself, but he wastes that which is wanted for the most noble use, and which Christ himself is ready to receive at his hands. And if we are angry at a poor man, and look upon him as a wretch, when he throws away that which should buy his own bread; how must we appear in the sight of God, if we make a wanton idle use of that, which should buy bread and clothes for the hungry and naked brethren, who are as near and dear to God as we are, and fellow-heirs of the same state of future glory? This is the spirit of Miranda, and thus she uses the gifts of God; she is only one of a certain number of poor people, that are relieved out of her fortune, and she only differs from them in the blessedness of giving.

Excepting her victuals, she never spent ten pounds a year upon herself. If you were to see her, you would wonder what poor body it was, that was so surprisingly neat and clean. She has but one rule that she observes in her dress, to be always clean, and in the cheapest things. Everything about her resembles the purity of her soul, and she is always clean without, because she is always pure within.

Every morning sees her early at her prayers; she rejoices in the beginning of every day, because it begins all her pious rules of holy living, and brings the fresh pleasure of repeating them. She seems to be as a guardian angel to those that dwell about her, with her watchings and prayers blessing the place where she dwells, and making intercession with God for those that are asleep.

Her devotions have had some intervals, and God has heard several of her private prayers before the light is suffered to enter into her sister's room. Miranda does not know what it is to have a dull half-day; the return of her hours of prayer, and her religious exercises, come too often to let any considerable part of time lie heavy upon her hands.

When you see her at work, you see the same wisdom that governs all her other actions, she is either doing something that is necessary for herself, or necessary for others, who want to be assisted. There is scarcely a poor family in the neighbourhood, but wears something or other that has had the labour of her hands. Her wise and pious mind neither wants the amusement, nor can bear the folly of idle and impertinent work. She can admit of no such folly as this in the day, because she is to answer for all her actions at night. When there is no wisdom to be observed in the employment of her hands, when there is no useful or charitable work to be done, Miranda will work no more. At her table she lives strictly by this rule of holy scripture, 'Whether ye eat, or drink, or whatsoever ye do, do all to the glory of God.' This makes her begin and end every meal, as she begins and ends every day, with acts of devotion: she eats and drinks only for the sake of living, and with so regular an abstinence, that every meal is an exercise of self-denial, and she humbles her body every time that she is forced to feed it. If Miranda were to run a race for her life, she would submit to a diet that was proper for it. But as the race which is set before her, is a race of holiness, purity, and heavenly affection, which she is to finish in a corrupt, disordered body of earthly passions, so her everyday diet has only this one end, to make her body fitter for this spiritual race. She does not weigh her meat in a pair of scales, but she weighs it in a much better balance; so much as gives a proper strength to her body, and renders it able and willing to obey the soul, to join in psalms and prayers, and lift up eyes and hands towards heaven with greater readiness, so much is Miranda's meal. So that Miranda will never have her eyes swell with fatness, or pant under a heavy load of flesh, until she has changed her religion.

The holy scriptures, especially of the New Testament, are her daily study; these she reads with a watchful attention, constantly casting an eye upon herself, and trying herself, by every doctrine that is there. When she has the New Testament in her hand, she supposes herself at the feet of our Saviour and his apostles, and makes everything that she learns of them, so many laws of her life. She receives their sacred words with as much attention, and reverence, as if she saw their persons, and knew that they were just come from heaven, on purpose to teach her the way that leads to it.

She thinks, that the trying of herself every day by the doctrines of scripture, is the only possible way to be ready for her trial at the last day. She is sometimes afraid that she lays out too much money in books, because she cannot forbear buying all practical books of any note; especially such as enter into the heart of religion, and describe the inward holiness of the Christian life. But of all human writings, the lives of pious persons, and eminent saints, are her greatest delight. In these she searches as for hidden treasure, hoping to find some secret of holy living, some uncommon degree of piety, which she may make her own. By this means Miranda has her head and her heart so stored with all the principles of wisdom and holiness, she is so full of the one main business of life, that she finds it difficult to converse upon any other subject; and if you are in her company, when she thinks it proper to talk, you must be made wiser and better, whether you will or no.

To relate her charity, would be to relate the history of every day for twenty years; for so long has all her fortune been spent that way. She has set up nearly twenty poor tradesmen that had failed in their business, and saved as many from failing. She has educated several poor children, that were picked up in the streets, and put them in a way of an honest employment. As soon as any labourer is confined at home with sickness, she sends him, till he recovers, twice the value of his wages, that he may have one part to give to his family, as usual, and the other to provide things convenient for his sickness.

If a family seems too large to be supported by the labour of those that can work in it, she pays their rent, and gives them something yearly towards their clothing. By this means, there are many poor families that live in a comfortable manner, and are from year to year blessing her in their prayers.

If there is any poor man or woman, that is more than ordinarily wicked and reprobate, Miranda has her eyes upon them, she watches their time of need and adversity; and if she can discover that they are in any great straits, or affliction, she gives them speedy relief. She has this care for this sort of people, because she once saved a very profligate person from being carried to prison, who immediately became a true penitent.

There is nothing in the character of Miranda more to be admired, than this temper. For this tenderness of affection towards the most abandoned sinners, is the highest instance of a divine and God-like soul.

Miranda once passed by a house, where the man and his wife were cursing and swearing at one another, in a most dreadful manner, and three children crying about them; this sight so much affected her compassionate mind, that she went the next day, and bought the three children, that they might not be ruined by living with such wicked parents; they now live with Miranda, are blessed with her care and prayers, and all the good works which she can do for them. They hear her talk, they see her live, they join with her in psalms and prayers. The eldest of them has already converted his parents from their wicked life, and shows a turn of mind so remarkably pious, that Miranda intends him for holy orders; that being thus saved himself, he may be zealous in the salvation of souls, and do to other miserable objects, as she has done to him.

Miranda is a constant relief to poor people in their misfortunes and accidents; there are sometimes little misfortunes that happen to them, which of themselves they could never be able to overcome. The death of a cow, or a horse, or some little robbery, would keep them in distress all their lives. She does not suffer them to grieve under such accidents as these. She immediately gives them the full value of their loss, and makes use of it as a means of raising their minds towards God.

She has a great tenderness for old people that are grown past their labour. The parish allowance to such people is very seldom a comfortable maintenance. For this reason they are the constant objects of her care; she adds so much to their allowance, as somewhat exceeds the wages they got when they were young. This she does to comfort the infirmities of their age, that being free from trouble and distress, they may serve God in peace, and tranquillity of mind. She has generally a large number of this kind, who by her charities and exhortations to holiness, spend their last days in great piety and devotion.

Miranda never wants compassion, even to common beggars; especially towards those that are old or sick, or full of sores, that want eyes or limbs. She hears their complaints with tenderness, gives them some proof of her kindness, and never rejects them with hard, or reproachful language, for fear of adding affliction to her fellow-creatures.

If a poor old traveller tells her, that he has neither strength, nor food, nor money left, she never bids him go to the place from whence he came, or tells him, that she cannot relieve him, because he may be a cheat, or she does not know him; but she relieves him for that reason, because he is a stranger, and unknown to her. For it is the most noble part of charity, to be kind and tender to those whom we never saw before, and perhaps never may see again in this life. I was a stranger, and ye took me in, saith our blessed Saviour; but who can perform this duty, that will not relieve persons that are unknown to him?

Miranda considers, that Lazarus was a common beggar, that he was the care of angels, and carried into Abraham's bosom. She considers, that our blessed Saviour and his apostles, were kind to beggars; that they spoke comfortably to them, healed their diseases, and restored eyes and limbs to the lame and blind. That Peter said to the beggar that wanted an alms from him, 'Silver and gold have I none, but such as I have give I thee; in the name of Jesus Christ of Nazareth, rise up and walk.' Miranda, therefore, never treats beggars with disregard and aversion, but she imitates the kindness of our Saviour and his apostles towards them; and though she cannot, like them, work miracles for their relief, yet she relieves them with that power that she hath; and may say with the apostle, 'Such as I have give I thee, in the name of Jesus Christ.'

It may be, says Miranda, that I may often give to those that do not deserve it, or that will make an ill use of my alms. But what then? Is not this the very method of divine goodness? Does not God make his sun to rise on the evil, and on the good? Is not this the very goodness that is recommended to us in scripture, that by imitating of it, we may be children of our Father which is in heaven, who sendeth rain on the just, and on the unjust? And shall I with-hold a little money, or food, from my fellow-creature, for fear he should not be good enough to receive it of me? Do I beg God to deal with me, not according to my merit, but according to his own great goodness; and shall I be so absurd, as to with-hold my charity from a poor brother, because he may perhaps not deserve it? Shall I use a measure towards him, which I pray God never to use towards me?

Besides, where has the scripture made merit the rule or measure of charity? On the contrary, the scripture saith, 'If thy enemy hunger, feed him, if he thirst, give him drink.'

Now this plainly teaches us, that the merit of persons is to be no rule of our charity, but that we are to do acts of kindness to those that least of all deserve it. For if I am to love and do good to my worst enemies; if I am to be charitable to them, notwithstanding all their spite and malice, surely merit is no measure of charity. If I am not to with-hold my charity from such bad people, and who are at the same time my enemies, surely I am not to deny alms to poor beggars, whom I neither know to be bad people, nor any way my enemies.

You will perhaps say, that by this means I encourage people to be beggars. But the same thoughtless objection may be made against all kinds of charities, for they may encourage people to depend upon them. The same may be said against forgiving our enemies, for it may encourage people to do us hurt. The same may be said even against the goodness of God, that by pouring his blessings on the evil and on the good, on the just and on the unjust, evil and unjust men are encouraged in their wicked ways. The same may be said against clothing the naked, or giving medicines to the sick, for that may encourage people to neglect themselves, and be careless of their health. But when the love of God dwelleth in you, when it has enlarged your heart, and filled you with bowels of mercy and compassion, you will make no more such objections as these.

When you are at any time turning away the poor, the old, the sick and helpless traveller, the lame, or the blind, ask yourself this question, Do I sincerely wish these poor creatures may be as happy as Lazarus, that was carried by angels into Abraham's bosom? Do I sincerely desire that God would make them fellow-heirs with me in eternal glory? Now if you search into your soul, you will find that there are none of these motions there, that you are wishing nothing of this. For it is impossible for anyone heartily to wish a poor creature so great a happiness, and yet not have a heart to give him a small alms. For this reason, says Miranda, as far as I can, I give to all, because I pray God to forgive all; and I cannot refuse an alms to those whom I pray God to bless, whom I wish to be partaker of eternal glory, but am glad to show some degree of love to such, as, I hope, will be the objects of the infinite Love of God. And if, as our Saviour has assured us, it be more blessed to give than to receive, we ought to look upon those that ask our alms, as so many friends and benefactors, that come to do us a greater good than they can receive, that come to exalt our virtue, to be witnesses of our charity, to be monuments of our love, to be our advocates with God, to be to us in Christ's stead, to appear for us at the day of judgment, and to help us to a blessedness greater than our alms can bestow on them.

This is the spirit, and this is the life of the devout Miranda; and if she lives ten years longer, she will have spent fifty hundred pounds in charity, for that which she allows herself, may fairly be reckoned amongst her alms.

When she dies, she must shine amongst apostles, and saints, and martyrs; she must stand amongst the first servants of God, and be glorious amongst those that have fought the good fight, and finished their course with joy.

CHAPTER XIV
CONCERNING THAT PART OF DEVOTION WHICH RELATES TO TIMES AND HOURS OF PRAYER. OF DAILY EARLY PRAYER IN THE MORNING. HOW WE ARE TO IMPROVE OUR FORMS OF PRAYER, AND HOW TO INCREASE THE SPIRIT OF DEVOTION.

Having in the foregoing chapter, shown the necessity of a devout spirit, or habit of mind in every part of our common life, in the discharge of all our business, in the use of all the gifts of God: I come now to consider that part of devotion, which relates to times and hours of prayer.

I take it for granted, that every Christian, that is in health, is up early in the morning; for it is much more reasonable to suppose a person up early, because he is a Christian, than because he is a labourer, or a tradesman, or a servant, or has business that wants him.

We naturally conceive some abhorrence of a man that is in bed, when he should be at his labour, or in his shop. We cannot tell how to think anything good of him, who is such a slave to drowsiness, as to neglect his business for it.

Let this therefore teach us to conceive, how odious we must appear in the sight of heaven, if we are in bed, shut up in sleep and darkness, when we should be praising God; and are such slaves to drowsiness, as to neglect our devotions for it.

For if he is to be blamed as a slothful drone, that rather chooses the lazy indulgence of sleep, than to perform his proper share of worldly business; how much more is he to be reproached, that had rather lie folded up in a bed, than be raising up his heart to God in acts of praise and adoration?

Prayer is the nearest approach to God, and the highest enjoyment of him, that we are capable of in this life.

*   *   *

I do not take upon me to prescribe to you the use of any particular forms of prayer, but only to show you the necessity of praying at such times, and in such a manner.

You will find here some helps, how to furnish yourself with such forms of prayer, as shall be useful to you. And if you are such a proficient in the spirit of devotion, that your heart is always ready to pray in its own language, in this case I press no necessity of borrowed forms.

For though I think a form of prayer very necessary and expedient for public worship, yet if anyone can find a better way of raising his heart unto God in private, than by prepared forms of prayer, I have nothing to object against it; my design being only to assist and direct such as stand in need of assistance.

Thus much, I believe, is certain, that the generality of Christians ought to use forms of prayer, at all the regular times of prayer. It seems right for everyone to begin with a form of prayer; and if in the midst of his devotions, he finds his heart ready to break forth into new and higher strains of devotion, he should leave his form for a while, and follow those fervours of his heart, till it again wants the assistance of his usual petitions.

This seems to be the true liberty of private devotion; it should be under the direction of some form; but not so tied down to it, but that it may be free to take such new expressions, as its present fervours happen to furnish it with; which sometimes are more affecting, and carry the soul more powerfully to God, than any expressions that were ever used before.

All people that have ever made any reflections upon what passes in their own hearts, must know that they are mighty changeable in regard to devotion. Sometimes our hearts are so awakened, have such strong apprehensions of the divine presence, are so full of deep compunction for our sins, that we cannot confess them in any language, but that of tears.

Sometimes the light of God's countenance shines so bright upon us, we see so far into the invisible world, we are so affected with the wonders of the love and goodness of God, that our hearts worship and adore in a language higher than that of words, and we feel transports of devotion, which can only be felt.

On the other hand, sometimes we are so sunk into our bodies, so dull and unaffected with that which concerns our souls, that our hearts are as much too low for our prayers; we cannot keep pace with our forms of confession, or feel half of that in our hearts which we have in our mouths; we thank and praise God with forms of words, but our hearts have little or no share in them.

It is therefore highly necessary, to provide against this inconstancy of our hearts, by having at hand such forms of prayer, as may best suit us when our hearts are in their best state, and also be most likely to raise and stir them up, when they are sunk into dulness. For as words have a power of affecting our hearts on all occasions, as the same thing differently expressed has different effects upon our minds; so it is reasonable, that we should make this advantage of language, and provide ourselves with such forms of expressions, as are most likely to move and enliven our souls, and fill them with sentiments suitable to them.

The first thing that you are to do, when you are upon your knees, is to shut your eyes, and with a short silence let your soul place itself in the presence of God; that is, you are to use this, or some other better method, to separate yourself from all common thoughts, and make your heart as sensible as you can of the divine presence.

Now if this recollection of spirit is necessary, as who can say it is not? then how poorly must they perform their devotions, who are always in a hurry; who begin them in haste, and hardly allow themselves time to repeat their very form, with any gravity or attention? Theirs is properly saying prayers, instead of praying.

To proceed; if you were to use yourself (as far as you can) to pray always in the same place; if you were to reserve that place for devotion, and not allow yourself to do anything common in it; if you were never to be there yourself, but in times of devotion; if any little room, (or if that cannot be) if any particular part of a room was thus used, this kind of consecration of it, as a place holy unto God, would have an effect upon your mind, and dispose you to such tempers, as would very much assist your devotion. For by having a place thus sacred in your room, it would in some measure resemble a chapel or house of God. This would dispose you to be always in the spirit of religion, when you were there; and fill you with wise and holy thoughts, when you were by yourself. Your own apartment would raise in your mind, such sentiments as you have, when you stand near an altar; and you would be afraid of thinking or doing anything that was foolish near that place, which is the place of prayer, and holy intercourse with God.

When you begin your petitions, use such various expressions of the attributes of God, as may make you most sensible of the greatness and power of the divine nature.

Begin therefore in words like these: 'O Being of all beings, Fountain of all light and glory, gracious Father of men and angels, whose universal Spirit is everywhere present, giving life, and light, and joy, to all angels in heaven, and all creatures upon earth,' &c.

For these representations of the divine attributes, which show us in some degree the majesty and greatness of God, are an excellent means of raising our hearts, into lively acts of worship and adoration.

What is the reason, that most people are so much affected with this petition in the burial service of our church: 'Yet, O Lord God most holy, O Lord most mighty, O holy and most merciful Saviour, deliver us not into the bitter pains of eternal death'? It is because the joining together of so many great expressions gives such a description of the greatness of the Divine Majesty, as naturally affects every sensible mind.

Although therefore prayer does not consist in fine words, or studied expressions; yet as words speak to the soul, as they have a certain power of raising thoughts in the soul; so those words which speak of God in the highest manner, which most fully express the power and presence of God, which raise thoughts in the soul most suitable to the greatness and providence of God, are the most useful, and most edifying in our prayers.

When you direct any of your petitions to our blessed Lord,

let it be in some expressions of this kind: 'O Saviour of the world, God of God, Light of Light; thou that art the Brightness of thy Father's Glory, and the express Image of his Person; thou that art the Alpha and Omega, the Beginning and End of all things; thou that hast destroyed the power of the devil, that hast overcome death; thou that art entered into the Holy of Holies, that sittest at the right hand of the Father, that art high above all thrones and principalities, that makest intercession for all the world; thou that art the judge of the quick and dead; thou that wilt speedily come down in thy Father's glory, to reward all men according to their works, be thou my light and my peace,' &c.

For such representations, which describe so many characters of our Saviour's nature and power, are not only proper acts of adoration, but will, if they are repeated with any attention, fill our hearts with the highest fervours of true devotion.

Again, if you ask any particular grace of our blessed Lord, let it be in some manner like this:

'O holy Jesus, Son of the most high God, thou that wert scourged at a pillar, stretched and nailed upon a cross, for the sins of the world, unite me to thy cross, and fill my soul with thy holy, humble, and suffering spirit. O Fountain of mercy, thou that didst save the thief upon the cross, save me from the guilt of a sinful life; thou that didst cast seven devils out of Mary Magdalene, cast out of my heart all evil thoughts, and wicked tempers. O Giver of life, thou that didst raise Lazarus from the dead, raise up my soul from the death and darkness of sin. Thou that didst give to thy apostles power over unclean spirits, give me power over my own heart. Thou that didst appear unto thy disciples when the doors were shut, do thou appear unto me in the secret apartment of my heart. Thou that didst cleanse the lepers, heal the sick, and give sight to the blind, cleanse my heart, heal the disorders of my soul, and fill me with heavenly light.'

Now these kinds of appeals have a double advantage; first, as they are so many proper acts of our faith, whereby we not only show our belief of the miracles of Christ, but turn them at the same time into so many instances of worship and adoration.

Secondly, as they strengthen and increase the faith of our

prayers, by presenting to our minds so many instances of that power and goodness, which we call upon for our own assistance.

For he that appeals to Christ, as casting out devils, and raising the dead, has then a powerful motive in his mind to pray earnestly, and depend faithfully upon his assistance.

Again; in order to fill your prayers with excellent strains of devotion, it may be of use to you to observe this further rule:

When at any time either in reading the scripture, or any book of piety, you meet with a passage, that more than ordinarily affects your mind, and seems as it were to give your heart a new motion towards God, you should try to turn it into the form of a petition, and then give it a place in your prayers. By this means, you would be often improving your prayers, and storing yourself with proper forms, of making the desires of your heart known unto God.

At all the stated hours of prayer, it will be of great benefit to you, to have something fixed, and something at liberty, in your devotions.

You should have some fixed subject, which is constantly to be the chief matter of your prayer at that particular time; and yet have liberty to add such other petitions, as your condition may then require.

For instance; as the morning is to you the beginning of a new life; as God has then given you a new enjoyment of yourself, and a fresh entrance into the world, it is highly proper, that your first devotions should be a praise and thanksgiving to God, as for a new creation; and that you should offer and devote body and soul, all that you are, and all that you have, to his service and glory.

Receive therefore every day, as a resurrection from death, as a new enjoyment of life; meet every rising sun with such sentiments of God's goodness, as if you had seen it, and all things new created upon your account; and under the sense of so great a blessing, let your joyful heart praise and magnify so good and glorious a Creator.

Let therefore praise and thanksgiving, and oblation of yourself unto God, be always the fixed and certain subject of your first prayers in the morning; and then take the liberty of adding such other devotions, as the accidental difference of your state, or the accidental difference of your heart, shall then make most needful and expedient for you.

For one of the greatest benefits of private devotion consists in rightly adapting our prayers to these two conditions, the difference of our state, and the difference of our hearts.

By the difference of our state is meant the difference of our external state or condition, as of sickness, health, pains, losses, disappointments, troubles, particular mercies, or judgments from God; all sorts of kindnesses, injuries or reproaches from other people.

Now as these are great parts of our state of life, as they make great difference in it, by continually changing; so our devotion will be made doubly beneficial to us, when it watches to receive and sanctify all these changes of our state, and turns them all into so many occasions, of a more particular application to God, of such thanksgivings, such resignation, such petitions, as our present state more especially requires.

And he that makes every change in his state, a reason of presenting unto God some particular petitions suitable to that change, will soon find, that he has taken an excellent means, not only of praying with fervour, but of living as he prays.

The next condition, to which we are always to adapt some part of our prayers, is the difference of our hearts; by which is meant the different state of the tempers of our hearts, as of love, joy, peace, tranquillity; dulness and dryness of spirit, anxiety, discontent, motions of envy and ambition, dark and disconsolate thoughts, resentments, fretfulness, and peevish tempers.

Now as these tempers, through the weakness of our nature, will have their succession more or less, even in pious minds; so we should constantly make the present state of our heart, the reason of some particular application to God.

If we are in the delightful calm of sweet and easy passions, of love and joy in God, we should then offer the grateful tribute of thanksgiving to God, for the possession of so much happiness, thankfully owning and acknowledging him as the bountiful Giver of it all.

If, on the other hand, we feel ourselves laden with heavy passions, with dulness of spirit, anxiety and uneasiness, we must then look up to God in acts of humility, confessing our unworthiness, opening our troubles to him, beseeching him in his good time to lessen the weight of our infirmities, and to deliver us from such passions as oppose the purity and perfection of our souls.

Now by thus watching, and attending to the present state of our hearts, and suiting some of our petitions exactly to their wants, we shall not only be well acquainted with the disorders of our souls, but also be well exercised in the method of curing them.

By this prudent and wise application of our prayers, we shall get all the relief from them that is possible; and the very changeableness of our hearts will prove a means of exercising a greater variety of holy tempers.

Now by all that has here been said, you will easily perceive, that persons careful of the greatest benefit of prayer, ought to have a great share in the forming and composing their own devotions.

As to that part of their prayers, which is always fixed to one certain subject, in that they may use the help of forms composed by other persons; but in that part of their prayers, which they are always to suit to the present state of their life, and the present state of their heart, there they must let the sense of their own condition help them to such kinds of petition, thanksgiving, or resignation, as their present state more especially requires.

Happy are they, who have this business and employment upon their hands!

And now, if people of leisure, whether men, or women, who are so much at a loss how to dispose of their time, who are forced into poor contrivances, idle visits, and ridiculous diversions, merely to get rid of hours that hang heavily upon their hands; if such were to appoint some certain spaces of their time, to the study of devotion, searching after all the means and helps to attain a devout spirit; if they were to collect the best forms of devotion, to use themselves to transcribe the finest passages of scripture-passages; if they were to collect the devotions, confessions, petitions, praises, resignations, and thanksgivings, which are scattered up and down in the psalms, and range them under proper heads, as so much proper fuel for the flame of their own devotion; if their minds were often thus employed, sometimes meditating upon them, sometimes getting them by heart, and making them as habitual as their own thoughts, how fervently would they pray, who came thus prepared to prayer?

And how much better would it be, to make this benefit of leisure-time, than to be dully and idly lost in the poor impertinences of a playing, visiting, wandering life?

How much better would it be, to be thus furnished with hymns and anthems of the saints, and teach their souls to ascend to God, than to corrupt, bewilder, and confound their hearts, with the wild fancies, the lustful thoughts of a lewd poet?

Now though people of leisure seem called more particularly to this study of devotion, yet persons of much business or labour must not think themselves excused from this, or some better method of improving their devotion.

For the greater their business is, the more need they have of some such method as this, to prevent its power over their hearts; to secure them from sinking into worldly tempers, and preserve a sense and taste of heavenly things in their minds. And a little time regularly and constantly employed to any one use or end, will do great things, and produce mighty effects.

And it is for want of considering devotion in this light, as something that is to be nursed and cherished with care, as something that is to be made part of our business, that is to be improved with care and contrivance, by art and method, and a diligent use of the best helps; it is for want of considering it in this light, that so many people are so little benefited by it, and live and die strangers to that spirit of devotion, which by a prudent use of proper means, they might have enjoyed in a high degree.

For though the spirit of devotion is the gift of God, and not attainable by any mere power of our own, yet it is mostly given, and never withheld, from those, who by a wise and diligent use of proper means, prepare themselves for the reception of it.

And it is amazing to see, how eagerly men employ their parts, their sagacity, time, study, application and exercise; how all helps are called to their assistance, when anything is intended and desired in worldly matters; and how dull, negligent, and unimproved they are, how little they use their parts, sagacity, and abilities, to raise and increase their devotion!

Mundanus is a man of excellent parts, and clear apprehension. He is well advanced in age, and has made a great figure in business. Every part of trade and business that has fallen in his way, has had some improvement from him; and he is always contriving to carry every method of doing anything well, to its greatest height. Mundanus aims at the greatest perfection in everything. The soundness and strength of his mind, and his just way of thinking upon things, makes him intent upon removing all imperfections.

He can tell you all the defects and errors in all the common methods, whether of trade, building, or improving land, or manufactures. The clearness and strength of his understanding, which he is constantly improving, by continual exercise in these matters, by often digesting his thoughts in writing, and trying everything every way, has rendered him a great master of most concerns in human life.

Thus has Mundanus gone on, increasing his knowledge and judgment, as fast as his years came upon him.

The one only thing which has not fallen under his improvement, nor received any benefit from his judicious mind, is his devotion: this is just in the same poor state it was, when he was only six years of age, and the old man prays now, in that little form of words, which his mother used to hear him repeat night and morning.

This Mundanus, that hardly ever saw the poorest utensil, or ever took the meanest trifle into his hand, without considering how it might be made, or used to better advantage, has gone all his life long praying in the same manner, as when he was a child; without ever considering how much better or oftener he might pray; without considering how improvable the spirit of devotion is, how many helps a wise and reasonable man may call to his assistance, and how necessary it is, that our prayers should be enlarged, varied and suited to the particular state and condition of our lives.

If Mundanus sees a book of devotion, he passes it by, as he does a spelling-book, because he remembers that he learned to pray, so many years ago under his mother, when he learned to spell.

Now how poor and pitiable is the conduct of this man of sense, who has so much judgment and understanding in everything, but that which is the whole wisdom of man?

And how miserably do many people, more or less, imitate this conduct?

All of which seems to be owing to a strange infatuated state of negligence, which keeps people from considering what devotion is. For if they did but once proceed so far as to reflect about it, or ask themselves any questions concerning it, they would soon see, that the spirit of devotion was like any other sense or understanding, that is only to be improved by study, care, application, and the use of such means and helps, as are necessary to make a man proficient in any art or science.

Classicus is a man of learning and well versed in all the best authors of antiquity. He has read them so much, that he has entered into their spirit, and can very ingeniously imitate the manner of any of them. All their thoughts are his thoughts, and he can express himself in their language. He is so great a friend to this improvement of the mind, that if he lights on a young scholar, he never fails to advise him concerning his studies.

Classicus tells this young man, he must not think that he has done enough, when he has learned only languages; but that he must be daily conversant with the best authors, read them again and again, catch their spirit by living with them, and that there is no other way of becoming like them, or of making himself a man of taste and judgment.

How wise might Classicus have been, and how much good might he have done in the world, if he had but thought as justly of devotion, as he does of learning?

He never, indeed, says anything shocking or offensive about

devotion, because he never thinks, or talks about it. It suffers nothing from him, but neglect and disregard.

The two testaments would not have had so much as a place amongst his books, but that they are both to be had in Greek.

Classicus thinks that he sufficiently shows his regard for the Holy Scripture, when he tells you, that he has no other books of piety besides them.

It is very well, Classicus, that you prefer the bible to all other books of piety; he has no judgment, that is not thus far of your opinion.

But if you will have no other book of piety besides the bible, because it is the best, how comes it, Classicus, that you do not content yourself with one of the best books amongst the Greeks and Romans? How comes it that you are so greedy and eager after all of them? How comes it that you think the knowledge of one is a necessary help to the knowledge of the other? How comes it that you are so earnest, so laborious, so expensive of your time and money, to restore broken periods, and scraps of the ancients?

How comes it that you read so many commentators upon Cicero, Horace, and Homer, and not one upon the Gospel? How comes it that your love of Cicero, and Ovid, makes you love to read an author that writes like them; and yet your esteem for the Gospel gives you no desire, nay, prevents your reading such books, as breathe the very spirit of the Gospel?

How comes it that you tell your young scholar, he must not content himself with barely understanding his authors, but must be continually reading them all, as the only means of entering into their spirit, and forming his own judgment according to them?

Why then must the bible lie alone in your study? Is not the spirit of the saints, the piety of the holy followers of Jesus Christ, as good and necessary a means of entering into the spirit and taste of the gospel, as the reading of the ancients is of entering into the spirit of antiquity?

Is the spirit of poetry only to be got by much reading of poets and orators? And is not the spirit of devotion to be got in the same way, by frequently reading the holy thoughts, and pious strains of devout men?

Is your young poet in search after every line, that may give new wings to his fancy, or direct his imagination? And is it not as reasonable for him, who desires to improve in the divine life, that is, in the love of heavenly things, to search after every strain of devotion, that may move, kindle, and inflame the holy ardour of his soul?

Do you advise your orator to translate the best orations, to commit much of them to memory, to be frequently exercising his talent in this manner, that habits of thinking and speaking justly may be formed in his mind? And is there not the same benefit and advantage to be made by books of devotion? Should not a man use them in the same way, that habits of devotion, and aspiring to God in holy thoughts, may be well formed in his soul?

Now the reason why Classicus does not think and judge thus reasonably of devotion, is owing to his never thinking of it in any other manner, than as the repeating a form of words. It never in his life entered into his head, to think of devotion as a state of the heart, as an improvable talent of the mind, as a temper that is to grow and increase like our reason and judgment, and to be formed in us by such a regular diligent use of proper means, as are necessary to form any other wise habit of mind.

And it is for want of this, that he has been content all his life, with the bare letter of prayer, and eagerly bent upon entering into the spirit of heathen poets and orators.

And it is much to be lamented, that numbers of scholars are more or less chargeable with this excessive folly; so negligent of improving their devotion, and so desirous of other poor accomplishments, as they thought it a nobler talent, to be able to write an epigram in the turn of Martial, than to live, and think, and pray to God, in the spirit of St. Austin.

And yet, to correct this temper, and fill a man with a quite contrary spirit, there seems to be no more required, than the bare belief in the truth of Christianity.

And if you were to ask Mundanus, and Classicus, or any man of business, or learning, whether piety is not the highest perfection of man, or devotion the greatest attainment in the world, they must both be forced to answer in the affirmative, or else give up the truth of the gospel.

For to set any accomplishment against devotion, or to think anything, or all things in the world, can bear any proportion to its excellency, is the same absurdity in a Christian, as it would be in a philosopher to prefer a meal's meat, to the greatest improvement in knowledge.

For as philosophy professes purely the search and enquiry after knowledge, so Christianity supposes, intends, desires, and aims at nothing else, but the raising fallen man to a divine life, to such habits of holiness, such degrees of devotion, as may fit him to enter among the holy inhabitants of the kingdom of heaven.

He that does not believe this of Christianity, may be reckoned an infidel; and he that believes thus much, has faith enough to give him a right judgment of the value of things, to support him in a sound mind, and enable him to conquer all the temptations which the world shall lay in his way.

To conclude this chapter, devotion is nothing else but right apprehensions and right affections towards God.

All practices therefore that heighten and improve our true apprehensions of God, all ways of life that tend to nourish, raise, and fix our affections upon him, are to be reckoned so many helps and means to fill us with devotion.

As prayer is the proper fuel of this holy flame, so we must use all our care and contrivance to give prayer its full power; as by alms, self-denial, frequent retirements, and holy readings, composing forms for ourselves, or using the best we can get, adding length of time, and observing hours of prayer; changing, improving, and suiting our devotions to the condition of our lives, and the state of our hearts.

Those who have most leisure, seem more especially called to a more eminent observance of these holy rules of a devout life. And they who by the necessity of their state, and not through their own choice, have but little time to employ thus, must make the best use of that little they have.

For this is the certain way of making devotion produce a devout life.

The Grounds and Reasons of Christian Regeneration

Man was created by God after his own image, and in his own likeness, a living mirror of the divine nature: where Father, Son, and Holy Ghost, each brought forth their own nature in a creaturely manner.

As the Son, who is begotten of the Father, is the brightness of the Father's glory, and the Holy Ghost proceedeth from the Father and the Son, as an amiable, moving life of both; so it was in this created image of the Holy Trinity. In it, the Father's nature generated the nature of the Son, and the Holy Ghost proceeded from them both, as an amiable, moving life of both. This was the likeness or image of God, in which the first man was created, a true offspring of God, in whom the divine birth sprung up as in the Deity, where Father, Son, and Holy Ghost saw themselves in a creaturely manner.

In the divine nature the Father cannot possibly be separated from the Son, nor the Holy Ghost from both, or either of them. But such separation could come to pass in the Trinity, become creaturely, or in the created living image of the Trinity.

If such separation could not have happened, man could not have fallen out of paradise; for so long as this image of the Holy Trinity continued unbroken, so long it must be in paradise, heaven, or the kingdom of divine joy.

But that this separation could happen in this created image of the Trinity, viz., that the birth of the Son, and the arising or proceeding of the Holy Ghost, could be separated or lost, is also certain; because man is actually fallen out of paradise into this poor, wretched, perishable world.

Whilst man continued in an unbroken image of the Holy Trinity, he was necessarily in paradise, in the open enjoyment of the kingdom of God. He stood indeed upon the earth, and with the same outward world about him, as we do now; but paradise was over all, the cover of all; and therefore he neither saw nor felt either his own outward body, or the things of this outward world, in the manner, as we now see, and feel them. His own dark, gross, heavy, fleshly body, which appeared after the fall, and the naked grossness, heaviness, darkness, discord, contrariety, and enmity, of the elements of this outward world, the strife of heat and cold, of storms and tempests, were things suppressed in paradise, and as entirely hid from his eyes, as the darkness of the night is hid from our eyes by the light of the day.

*   *   *

Our baptism is to signify our seeking and obtaining a new birth. And our being baptized in, or into the name of the Father, Son, and Holy Ghost, tells us in the plainest manner, what birth it is that we seek, namely, such a new birth as may make us again what we were at first, a living real image or offspring of the Father, Son, and Holy Ghost.

It is owned on all hands, that we are baptized into a renovation of some divine birth that we had lost; and that we may not be at a loss to know what that divine birth is, the form in baptism openly declares to us, that it is to regain that first birth of Father, Son, and Holy Ghost in our souls, which at the first made us to be truly and really images of the nature of the Holy Trinity in Unity. The form in baptism is but very imperfectly apprehended, till it is understood to have this great meaning in it. And it must be owned, that the scriptures tend wholly to guide us to this understanding of it. For since they teach us a birth of God, a birth of the Spirit, that we must obtain, and that baptism, the appointed sacrament of this new birth, is to be done in the name of the Father, Son, and Holy Ghost, can there be any doubt, that this sacrament is to signify the renovation of the birth of the Holy Trinity in our souls? And that therefore this was the holy image born or created at first, when God said, 'Let us make man in our image, after our own likeness,' that is, so make him, that we may see ourselves, our own nature in him, in a creaturely manner.

What an harmonious agreement does there thus appear, between our creation and redemption? and how finely, how surprisingly do our first and our second birth answer to, and illustrate one another?

At our first birth it is said thus, 'Let us make Man in our image, after our own likeness'; when the divine birth was lost, and man was to receive it again, it is said, 'Be thou baptized into the name of the Father, Son, and Holy Ghost': which is saying, 'Let the divine birth, be brought forth again in thee, or be thou born again such an image of Father, Son, and Holy Ghost, as thou wast at first.'

These considerations all taken from the plain words, and acknowledged doctrines of scripture, do, I think, sufficiently declare and prove to us, these great truths of the last importance, namely, that the image in which man was created, was such, as in which, the Holy Trinity saw itself, or its own nature in a creaturely manner, in which the Father's nature generated the nature of the Son, and the Holy Ghost proceeded from them both, as the amiable moving life of both.

That by Adam's sin, this holy image of the Holy Trinity was broken, and in such a manner, that the birth of the Son of God, and of the Holy Spirit, was no more in it, and that therefore in a stupendous mystery of love, the Son of God united himself to our fallen nature, to recover, and restore to it, all that it had lost, and in such a manner, that it might never be lost again to all eternity.

As soon as it is observed and known, that our fall consisted in the losing of the birth of the Son of God in our soul, and consequently the proceeding forth of the Holy Spirit in it, there appears a surprising agreeableness and fitness, in the means of our redemption, namely, that we could only be saved by the eternal Son of God; that he only could save us, by taking our nature upon him, and so uniting it with him, that his life, or birth might again arise in us, as at the first, and so we become again a perfect living image of the Holy Trinity.

Now the reason why I have gone thus far in inquiring into the dignity of man's original state, and searched thus deep into his lamentable fall, is this, to point out to the reader the true nature of the Christian religion, and the infinite importance of it; which religion is administered by God, as our only relief from our sad condition; and that he may at one view see the height and depth of divine love, which has had so great care of mankind.

I persuade myself, no one can see these truths, in the manner that I have represented them, without being in some degree inclined to believe them; and in the same degree stirred up to act in conformity to them.

We know nothing truly of the nature of the Christian religion, and our deep concern in it, but so far as we see into the nature of our first state in the creation, and our present state by the fall. And as this knowledge is in some degree necessary, so is it also in some degree obvious to every man.

Every man has a consciousness within himself, that a perfection in all kinds of virtue becomes him; this consciousness obliges him to set the best foot forwards, and to put on the appearance of all the virtue that he can. Now what else is this, but an inward strong testimony of his own mind, declaring to him, that perfection was his first state, and that because his nature once had it, he can neither lose the agreeable idea of it, nor quit his pretences to it; so that every man carries in his own breast, in the depth of his own frame and constitution, a strong proof of all those truths, that I have deduced from scripture. For I have not been speaking of things foreign or strange to us, but of things sensible felt within us, and spoken to us, by the whole form of our nature.

The condition in which I have represented our soul to be by the fall, a mere dark fire-breath, of an hellish nature, showing itself in every man more or less by its fruits, by such eruptions and breakings forth of dark passions, but hiding itself under an outward appearance of good, and a feigned civility or rectitude of manners, is what every man must be forced to own to be more or less in himself.

For this is the state of every man's soul, because it has lost the birth of the Son of God in it, and so is only as a strong root of a fiery life, unenlightened, and unblessed by that holy Word, which is the brightness of the Father's glory.

This dark root of a fiery, self-tormenting life, which is the whole nature of the fallen soul, destitute of the birth of the Son of God in it, is a life that subsists in four elements, as the life of this world hath its four elements.

Now the four elements of this dark, fiery soul, or fallen nature, are, (1.) a restless selfishness; (2.) a restless envy; (3.) a restless

Pride; and, (4.) a restless wrath or anger. I call them the elements
of the fallen soul, because they are that to it, which the four
elements of this world are to the life of the body.

Now these four elements which nourish and keep up the life
of the fallen soul, are also the four elements of hell, in which the
devils dwell; they can no more depart from, or exist out of these
elements, than an earthly life can depart from, or exist without
the four elements of this world, fire, air, water, and earth.

Now, as the soul, by the losing of the birth of the Son of God
in it, is become an aching dark root of fire, that has this restless
selfishness, restless envy, restless pride, and restless wrath in it,
which are the four elements of hell; so by its being in these, or
having them in it, it is come to pass, that evil spirits have such
communion with it, and so great power over it.

Every stirring of the soul in the element of pride, is a moving
in the devil's element, where he is, and has power to join and
act with it; every motion in the element of envy or wrath, is so
far impowering him to enter into the breath of our life, and settle
his fiery kingdom in us.

And thus in every one of these four elements, so far as we
willingly are in their sphere of activity, and act and stir according
to them, so far we become members of the devil's kingdom, and
have him for our leader, and guide. How watchful therefore
ought we to be of our hearts, how fearful of consenting to, or
not enough resisting every motion of these elements within us,
since every voluntary yielding to them, is opening the kingdom
of darkness in our souls, and giving the devil power to infuse
his wretched nature into us. And we have still further reason for
this fear and watchfulness, if it be considered, that as no one of
the elements of this outward world could be, or subsist, if the
other three were not, because they are the mutual cause of one
another; so it is in these other elements, if we live in one, we live
in all; selfishness cannot be, or subsist without envy, nor pride
without wrath and selfishness, nor any one of the four, without
carrying the other three in its bosom; therefore we must have the
same fear of any one, as of them all, for the name of every one
is legion.

Could we see, as we see outward objects, what a dreadful misery these four elements bring upon our souls, we should shun and fly from everything that gave life and strength to them, with more earnestness, than from the most violent evils that could threaten our bodies; we should choose to burn in any fire, rather than in that of our own wrath and pride, any poverty of outward life, rather than that of our own pinching envy, any prison, rather than to be shut up in our own dark selfishness. For all outward fires, chains, torments, slaveries, poverties, are but transient shadows of the tormenting, fiery, dark slavery of an unredeemed soul left, and given up to these four elements of hell.

And the reason why they are not a hell to profligate men now upon earth, is, as has been said, because we now live in flesh and blood, under the cheering influences of the sun, and the diversion and amusement of outward things, and in several forms of happiness, which our imaginations play with in time. This wandering of the imagination through its own inventions of delight, hinders the poor soul from feeling what it is, in its own nature; and therefore, though ever so much a slave of these elements, it only feels or perceives the torment of them by fits, and on certain occasions. And yet sometimes it is seen, that one or other of these elements awakens so violently, as to become intolerable, and to give a true and plain foretaste of the condition and nature of hell in the soul that feels it.

Here again, I cannot help observing by-the-by, the wondrous excellency and divine nature of the gospel religion, which knowing our fall to consist in this darkened fire of the soul, dwelling in these elements of hell, has set before us such amazing representations of humility, meekness, and universal love, as the imagination of man could never have thought of; namely, the humility, meekness, and lowliness of the Son of God, who left his glory, to take upon him the form of a servant for our sakes; the great love of God towards us sinners, in giving his only begotten Son to redeem us, and the love of God the Son, in laying his life down for us, that we might imitate this amazing humility, meekness, and divine love, and love one another as he has loved us. These are mysteries of love and mercy that are set before us, to quench the fiery wrath of our fallen nature, and to compel us, if possible, to abhor our own dark passions, and in humility and meekness become lovers of God, and one another.

Now so far as we, by true resignation to God, die to the element of selfishness and own will, so far as by universal love, we die to the element of envy, so far as by humility we die to the element of pride, so far as by meekness we die to the element of wrath, so far we get away from the devil, enter into another kingdom, and leave him to dwell without us in his own elements.

These are not fictions of a visionary imagination, but sober truths, spoken by the Word of God in scripture, and written and engraven in the book of every man's own nature.

No man since the fall, but is a living witness to these truths; to deny them, is to own and prove them: for we could not tell a lie, or resist the truth, but because we have this dark enemy to truth hidden in our bosom.

Now the greatest good that any man can do to himself, is to give leave to this inward deformity to show itself, and not to strive by any art or management, either of negligence or amusement, to conceal it from him. First, because this root of a dark fire-life within us, which is of the nature of hell, with all its elements of selfishness, envy, pride, and wrath, must be in some sort discovered to us, and felt by us, before we can enough feel, and enough groan under the weight of our disorder. Repentance is but a kind of table-talk, till we see so much of the deformity of our inward nature, as to be in some degree frightened and terrified at the sight of it. There must be some kind of an earthquake within us, something that must rend and shake us to the bottom, before we can be enough sensible, either of the state of death we are in, or enough desirous of that Saviour, who alone can raise us from it.

A plausible form of an outward life, that has only learned rules and modes of religion by use and custom, often keeps the soul for some time at ease, though all its inward root and ground of sin has never been shaken or molested, though it has never tasted of the bitter waters of repentance, and has only known the want of a Saviour by hearsay.

But things cannot pass thus: sooner or later, repentance must have a broken, and a contrite heart; we must with our blessed Lord go over the Brook Cedron, and with him sweat great drops of sorrow, before he can say for us, as he said for himself, 'It is finished.'

Now, though this sensibility of the sinfulness of our inward ground, is not to be expected to be the same in all, yet the truth and reality of it must, and will be in all, that do but give way to the discovery of it; and our sinfulness would ever be in our sight, if we did not industriously turn our eyes from it. If we used but half the pains, to find out the evil that is hidden in us, as we do to hide the appearance of it from others, we should soon find, that in the midst of our most orderly life, we are in death, and want a Saviour, to make our most apparent virtues to be virtuous.

It is therefore exceeding good and beneficial to us, to discover this dark, disordered fire of our soul; because when rightly known, and rightly dealt with, it can as well be made the foundation of heaven, as it is of hell.

For when the fire and strength of the soul is sprinkled with the blood of the Lamb, then its fire becomes a fire of light, and its strength is changed into a strength of triumphing love, and will be fitted to have a place amongst those flames of love, that wait about the throne of God.

The reason why we know so little of Jesus Christ, as our Saviour, atonement, and justification, why we are so destitute of that faith in him, which alone can change, rectify, and redeem our souls, why we live starving in the coldness and deadness of a formal, historical hearsay-religion, is this; we are strangers to our own inward misery and wants, we know not that we lie in the jaws of death and hell; we keep all things quiet within us, partly by outward forms, and modes of religion and morality, and partly by the comforts, cares and delights of this world. Hence it is that we consent to receive a Saviour, as we consent to admit of the four gospels, because only four are received by the church. We believe in a Saviour, not because we feel an absolute want of one, but because we have been told there is one, and that it would be a rebellion against God to reject him. We believe in Christ as our atonement, just as we believe that he cast seven devils out of Mary Magdalene, and so are no more helped, delivered, and justified by believing that he is our atonement, than by believing that he cured Mary Magdalene.

True faith is a coming to Jesus Christ to be saved, and delivered from a sinful nature, as the Canaanitish woman came to him, and would not be denied. It is a faith of love, a faith of hunger, a faith of thirst, a faith of certainty and firm assurance, that in love and longing, and hunger, and thirst, and full assurance, will lay hold on Christ, as its loving, assured, certain and infallible Saviour and atonement.

It is this faith, that breaks off all the bars and chains of death and hell in the soul; it is to this faith, that Christ always says what he said in the gospel, 'Thy faith hath saved thee, thy sins are forgiven thee; go in peace.' Nothing can be denied to this faith; all things are possible to it; and he that thus seeks Christ, must find him to be his salvation.

On the other hand, all things will be dull and heavy, difficult and impossible to us, we shall toil all the night and take nothing, we shall be tired with resisting temptations, grow old and stiff in our sins and infirmities, if we do not with a strong, full, loving, and joyful assurance, seek and come to Christ for every kind and degree of strength, salvation and redemption. We must come unto Christ, as the blind, the sick, and the leprous came to him, expecting all from him, and nothing from themselves. When we have this faith, then it is that Christ can do all his mighty works in us.

From the foregoing account anyone may be supposed already to see the nature and necessity of regeneration, or the new birth. It is as necessary as our salvation. By our fall, our soul has lost the birth of the Son of God in it; by this loss it is become a dark, wrathful, self-tormenting root of fire, shut up in the four hellish elements of selfishness, envy, pride, and wrath; considered as a fallen soul, it cannot stir one step, or exert one motion but in and according to these elements; therefore it is necessary to have this nature itself changed, and to be born again from above, as it is necessary to be delivered from hell, and eternal death.

For these elements are hell, and eternal death itself, and not without, or standing at a distance from us, but hell and death springing up in the forms, and essences of our fallen nature; they are the serpent that is in us, and constitute that gnawing worm which never dieth; for they mutually beget, and mutually torment each other, and so constitute a worm, or worming pain, that never dieth.

Now as this hell, serpent, worm, and death, are all within us, rising up in the forms and essences of our fallen soul; so our redeemer, or regenerator, whatever it be, must be also equally within us, and spring up from as great a depth in our nature. Now the scripture sufficiently tells us, that it is only the promised seed of the woman, the eternal Word, or Son of God made man, that can bruise this head, or kill this life of the serpent in us; therefore this seed of the woman must have its dwelling in the ground and essence of our nature, because the serpent is there, that a new life of a new nature may arise from this seed within us; and therefore it is plain that regeneration, or the new birth, is, and can be no other thing, but the recovering of the birth of the Son of God in the fallen soul.

And this is what the scripture means by the necessity of our being born of God, born again from above, born of the Spirit. Hence also we see in the clearest light the meaning of all those passages of scripture, where we are said to be in Christ, that Christ is in us; – that we must put on Christ; – that he must be formed in us; – that he is our life; – that we must eat his flesh and drink his blood; – that he is our atonement, that his blood alone cleanseth us from all our sins; that we have life from him, as the branches have life from the vine; – that he is our justification, or righteousness; that in him we are created again to good works; that without him we can do nothing, and have no life in us: all these, I say, and the like sayings of scripture, have a wonderful congruity and plainness in them, and fill the mind with the most excellent and solid truths, as soon as it is known, that regeneration is absolutely necessary, and that this regeneration signifies the recovering of the birth of the Son of God in the soul.

And as it does this justice to so great and concerning a part of scripture, so it sets the whole scheme of the Christian salvation in the most agreeable and engaging light, and such as is enough even to compel everyone, to embrace it with the utmost earnestness. The mystery of this salvation is still preserved, and yet hereby so unfolded, that every man has as much reason to desire to be born again, and to believe that the Son of God can only bring forth this birth in him, as to believe that God made him, and can alone make him happy.

A mediator, an atonement, regenerator, thus understood, must be as agreeable and desirable to every human mind, and as much according to his own wishes, as to be delivered from the uneasiness and disquiets of a nature, which he finds himself not master of, nor able to fix it in a state of better enjoyment.

What is it that any thoughtful, serious man could wish for, but to have a new heart, and a new spirit, free from the hellish, self-tormenting elements of selfishness, envy, pride, and wrath? His own experience has shown him, that nothing human can do this for him; can take away the root of evil that is in him; and it is so natural to him to think, that God alone can do it, that he has often been tempted to accuse God, for suffering it to be so with him.

Therefore to have the Son of God come from heaven to redeem him by a birth of his own divine nature in him, must be a way of salvation, highly suited to his own sense, wants and experience; because he finds, that his evil lies deep in the very essence and forms of his nature, and therefore can only be removed by the arising of a new birth, or life in the first essences of it.

Therefore an inward Saviour, a Saviour, that is God himself, raising his own divine birth in the fallen soul, has such an agreeableness and fitness in it, to do for him all that he wants, as must make every sober man, with open arms, ready and willing to receive such a salvation.

Some people have an idea, or notion of the Christian religion, as if God was thereby declared so full of wrath against fallen man, that nothing but the blood of his only begotten Son could satisfy his vengeance.

Nay, some have gone such lengths of wickedness, as to assert, that God had by immutable decrees reprobated, and rejected a great part of the race of Adam, to an inevitable damnation, to show forth and magnify the glory of his justice.

But these are miserable mistakers of the divine nature, and miserable reproachers of his great love, and goodness in the Christian dispensation.

For God is love, yea, all love, and so all love, that nothing but love can come from him; and the Christian religion, is nothing else but an open, full manifestation of his universal love towards all mankind.

As the light of the sun has only one common nature towards all objects that can receive it, so God has only one common nature of goodness, towards all created nature, breaking forth in infinite flames of love, upon every part of the creation, and calling everything to the highest happiness it is capable of.

God so loved man, when his fall was foreseen, that he chose him to salvation in Christ Jesus, before the foundation of the world. When man was actually fallen, God was so without all wrath towards him, so full of love for him, that he sent his only begotten Son into the world to redeem him. Therefore God has no nature towards man, but love, and all that he does to man, is love.

There is no wrath that stands between God and us, but what is awakened in the dark fire of our own fallen nature; and to quench this wrath, and not his own, God gave his only begotten Son to be made man. God has no more wrath in himself now, than he had before the creation, when he had only himself to love. The precious blood of his Son was not poured out to pacify himself (who in himself had no nature towards man but love), but it was poured out to quench the wrath and fire of the fallen soul, and kindle in it a birth of light, and love.

As man lives, and moves, and has his being in the divine nature, and is supported by it, whether his nature be good or bad; so the wrath of man, which was awakened in the dark fire of his fallen nature, may, in a certain sense, be called the wrath of God, as hell itself may be said to be in God, because nothing can be out of his immensity; yet this hell is not God, but the dark habitation of the devil. And this wrath which may be called the wrath of God, is not God, but the fiery wrath of the fallen soul.

And it was solely to quench this wrath, awakened in the human soul, that the blood of the Son of God was necessary, because nothing but a life and birth, derived from him into the human soul, could change this darkened root of a self-tormenting fire into an amiable image of the Holy Trinity, as it was at first created.

This was the wrath, vengeance, and vindictive justice that wanted to be satisfied, in order to our salvation; it was the wrath and fire of nature and creature kindled only in itself, by its departing from due resignation, and obedience to God.

When Adam and Eve went trembling behind the trees, through fear and dread of God, it was only this wrath of God awakened in them; it was a terror, and horror, and shivering of nature, that arose up in themselves, because the divine life, the birth of the Son of God, which is the brightness and joy of the soul, was departed from it, and had left it, to feel its own poor miserable state without it. And this may well enough be called the wrath, and justice of God upon them, because it was a punishment, or painful state of the soul, that necessarily followed their revolting from God.

But still there was no wrath, or painful sensation, that wanted to be appeased, or satisfied, but in nature and creature; it was only the wrath of fallen nature, that wanted to be changed into its first state of peace and love. When God spoke to them, he spoke only love; Adam, where art thou? And he called him, only to comfort him with a promised redemption, through a seed of the woman, a spark of the WORD of life which should reign in him, and his posterity, till all enemies were under their feet. God therefore is all love, and nothing but love and goodness can come from him. He is as far from anger in himself, as from pain and darkness. But when the fallen soul of man had awakened in itself, a wrathful, self-tormenting fire, which could never be put out by itself, which could never be relieved by the natural power of any creature whatsoever, then the Son of God, by a love, greater than that which created the world, became man, and gave his own blood, and life into the fallen soul, that it might through his life in it, be raised, quickened, and born again into its first state of inward peace and delight, glory and perfection, never to be lost any more. O inestimable truths! precious mysteries of the love of God, enough to split the hardest rock of the most obdurate heart, that is but able to receive one glimpse of them! Can the world resist such love as this? Or can any man doubt, whether he should open all that is within him to receive such a salvation?

O unhappy unbelievers, this mystery of love compels me in love, to call upon you, to beseech and entreat you, to look upon the Christian redemption in this amiable light. All the ideas that your own minds can form of love and goodness, must sink into nothing, as soon as compared with God's love and goodness in the redemption of mankind.

I appeal to nothing but the state of your own hearts and consciences, to prove the necessity of your embracing this mystery of divine love. I will grant you all that you can suppose, of the goodness of God, and that no creature will be finally lost, but what infinite love cannot save.

But still, here is no shadow of security for infidelity; and your refusing to be saved through the Son of God, whilst the soul is in the redeemable state of this life, may at the separation of the body, for aught you know, leave it in such a hell, as the infinite love of God cannot deliver it from. For, first, you have no kind, or degree of proof, that your soul is not that dark, self-tormenting, anguishing and imperishable fire, above-mentioned, which has lost its own proper light, and is only comforted by the light of the sun, till its redemption can be effected. Secondly, you have no kind, or degree of proof, that God himself can redeem, or save, or enlighten this dark fire-soul, any other way than, as the gospel proposes, by the birth of the Son of God in it. Therefore your own hearts must tell you, that for aught you know, infidelity, or the refusing of this birth of the Son of God, may, at the end of life, leave you in such a state of self-torment, as the infinite love of God can no way deliver you from.

You build much upon certain clear ideas, founded in the nature and fitness of things; but I beseech you to consider that here in this great point, on which all depends, you have no ideas at all; for you have not one clear, or even obscure idea, that your souls cannot be in this disordered state, or that they can be set into a right order, without the birth of the Son of God brought forth in them.

The Spirit of Prayer
Part One

CHAPTER II
DISCOVERING THE TRUE WAY OF TURNING TO GOD, AND OF FINDING THE KINGDOM OF HEAVEN, THE RICHES OF ETERNITY IN OUR SOULS

Thou hast seen, dear reader, the nature and necessity of regeneration; be persuaded therefore fully to believe, and firmly to settle in thy mind this most certain truth, that all our salvation consists in the manifestation of the nature, life, and spirit of Jesus Christ, in our inward new man. This alone is Christian redemption, this alone renews, and regains the first life of God in the soul of man. Every thing besides this is self, is fiction, is propriety, is own will, and however coloured, is only thy old man, with all his deeds. Enter therefore with all thy heart into this truth, let thy eye be always upon it, do every thing in view of it, try every thing by the truth of it, love nothing but for the sake of it. Wherever thou goest, whatever thou dost, at home, or abroad, in the field, or at church, do all in a desire of union with Christ, in imitation of his tempers and inclinations, and look upon all as nothing, but that which exercises and increases the spirit and life of Christ in thy soul. From morning to night keep Jesus in thy heart, long for nothing, desire nothing, hope for nothing, but to have all that is within thee changed into the spirit and temper of the holy Jesus. Let this be thy Christianity, thy church, and thy religion. For this new birth in Christ thus firmly believed, and continually desired, will do every thing that thou wantest to have done in thee; it will dry up all the springs of vice, stop all the workings of evil in thy nature, it will bring all that is good into thee, it will open all the gospel within thee, and thou wilt know what it is to be taught of God. This longing desire of thy heart to be one with Christ will soon put a stop to all the vanity of thy life, and nothing will be admitted to enter into thy heart, or proceed from it, but what comes from God and returns to God: thou wilt soon be, as it were, tied and bound in the chains of all holy affections and desires, thy mouth will have a watch set upon it, thy ears would willingly hear nothing that does not tend to God, nor thy eyes be open, but to see, and find occasions of doing good. In a word, when this faith has got both thy head and thy heart, it will then be with thee, as it was with the merchant who found a pearl of great price; it will make thee gladly to sell all that thou hast, and buy it. For all that had seized and possessed the heart of any man, whatever the merchant of this world had got together, whether of riches, power, honour, learning, or reputation, loses all its value, is counted but as dung, and willingly parted with, as soon as this glorious pearl, the new birth in Christ Jesus, is discovered and found by him. This therefore may serve as a touchstone, whereby every one may try the truth of his state; if the old man is still a merchant within thee, trading in all sorts of worldly honour, power, or learning, if the wisdom of this world is not foolishness to thee, if earthly interests, and sensual pleasures, are still the desire of thy heart, and only covered under a form of godliness, a cloak of creeds, observances, and institutions of religion, thou mayest be assured, that the pearl of great price is not yet found by thee. For where Christ is born, or his Spirit rises up in the soul, there all self is denied, and obliged to turn out; there all carnal wisdom, arts of advancement, with every pride and glory of this life, are as so many heathen idols all willingly renounced, and the man is not only content, but rejoices to say, that his kingdom is not of this world.

But thou wilt perhaps say, How shall this great work, the birth of Christ, be effected in me? It might rather be said, since Christ has an infinite power, and also an infinite desire to save mankind, how can anyone miss of this salvation, but through his own unwillingness to be saved by him? Consider, how was it, that the lame and blind, the lunatic and leper, the publican and sinner, found Christ to be their Saviour, and to do all that for them, which they wanted to be done to them? It was because they had a real desire of having that which they asked for, and therefore in true faith and prayer applied to Christ, that his Spirit and power might enter into them, and heal that which they wanted, and desired to be healed in them. Every one of these said in faith and desire, 'Lord, if thou wilt, thou canst make me whole.' And the answer was always this, 'According to thy faith, so be it done unto thee.' This is Christ's answer now, and thus it is done to every one of us at this day, as our faith is, so is it done unto us. And here lies the whole reason of our falling short of the salvation of Christ, it is because we have no will to it.

But you will say, Do not all Christians desire to have Christ to be their Saviour? Yes. But here is the deceit; all would have Christ to be their Saviour in the next world, and to help them into heaven when they die, by his power, and merits with God. But this is not willing Christ to be thy Saviour; for his salvation, if it is had, must be had in this world; if he saves thee, it must be done in this life, by changing and altering all that is within thee, by helping thee to a new heart, as he helped the blind to see, the lame to walk, and the dumb to speak. For to have salvation from Christ, is nothing else but to be made like unto him; it is to have his humility and meekness, his mortification and self-denial, his renunciation of the spirit, wisdom, and honours of this world, his love of God, his desire of doing God's will, and seeking only his honour. To have these tempers formed and begotten in thy heart, is to have salvation from Christ. But if thou willest not to have these tempers brought forth in thee, if thy faith and desire does not seek, and cry to Christ for them in the same reality, as the lame asked to walk, and the blind to see, then thou must be said to be unwilling to have Christ to be thy saviour.

Again, consider, how was it, that the carnal Jew, the deep-read scribe, the learned rabbi, the religious pharisee, not only did not receive, but crucified their Saviour? It was because they willed, and desired no such Saviour as he was, no such inward salvation as he offered to them. They desired no change of their own nature, no inward destruction of their own natural tempers, no deliverance from the love of themselves, and the enjoyments of their passions; they liked their state, the gratifications of their old man, their long robes, their broad phylacteries, and greetings in the markets. They wanted not to have their pride and self-love dethroned, their covetousness and sensuality to be subdued by a new nature from heaven derived unto them. Their only desire was the success of Judaism, to have an outward Saviour, a temporal prince, that should establish their law and ceremonies over all the earth. And therefore they crucified their dear Redeemer, and would have none of his salvation, because it all consisted in a change of their nature, in a new birth from above, and a kingdom of heaven to be opened within them by the Spirit of God.

Oh Christendom, look not only at the old Jews, but see thyself in this glass. For at this day (Oh sad truth to be told!) at this day, a Christ within us, an inward Saviour raising a birth of his own nature, life, and spirit within us, is rejected as gross enthusiasm, the learned rabbis take counsel against it. The propagation of Popery, the propagation of Protestantism, the success of some particular church, is the salvation which priests and people are chiefly concerned about.

But to return. It is manifest, that no one can fail of the benefit of Christ's salvation, but through an unwillingness to have it, and from the same spirit and tempers which made the Jews unwilling to receive it. But if thou wouldst still further know, how this great work, the birth of Christ, is to be effected in thee, then let this joyful truth be told thee, that this great work is already begun in every one of us. For this holy Jesus, that is to be formed in thee, that is to be the Saviour and new life of thy soul, that is to raise thee out of the darkness of death into the light of life, and give thee power to become a son of God, is already within thee, living, stirring, calling, knocking at the door of thy heart, and wanting nothing but thy own faith and good will, to have as real a birth and form in thee, as he had in the Virgin Mary. For the eternal Word, or Son of God, did not then first begin to be the Saviour of the world, when he was born in Bethlehem of Judea; but that Word which became man in the Virgin Mary, did, from the beginning of the world, enter as a Word of life, a Seed of salvation, into the first father of mankind, was inspoken into him, as an ingrafted Word, under the name and character of a bruiser of the serpent's head. Hence it is, that Christ said to his disciples, 'the Kingdom of God is within you'; that is, the divine nature is within you, given unto your first father, into the light of his life, and from him, rising up in the life of every son of Adam. Hence also the holy Jesus is said to be the 'Light, which lighteth every man that cometh into the world.' Not as he was born at Bethlehem, not as he had an human form upon earth; in these respects he could not be said to have been the light of every man that cometh into the world; but as he was that eternal Word, by which all things were created, which was the life and light of all things, and which had as a second Creator entered again into fallen man, as a bruiser of the serpent; in this respect it was truly said of our Lord, when on earth, that 'He was that light which lighteth every man, that cometh into the world.' For he was really and truly all this, as he was the Immanuel, the God with us, given unto Adam, and in him to all his offspring. See here the beginning and glorious extent of the Catholic Church of Christ, it takes in all the world. It is God's unlimited, universal mercy to all mankind; and every human creature, as sure as he is born of Adam, has a birth of the bruiser of the serpent within him, and so is infallibly in covenant with God through Jesus Christ. Hence also it is, that the holy Jesus is appointed to be judge of all the world, it is because all mankind, all nations and languages have in him and through him been put into covenant with God, and made capable of resisting the evil of their fallen nature.

When our blessed Lord conversed with the woman at Jacob's Well, he said unto her, 'If thou knewest the gift of God, and who it is that talketh with thee, thou wouldest have asked of him, and he would have given thee living water.' How happy (may anyone well say) was this woman of Samaria, to stand so near this gift of God, from whom she might have had living water, had she but vouchsafed to have asked for it! But, dear Christian, this happiness is thine; for this holy Jesus, the gift of God, first given unto Adam, and in him to all that are descended from him, is the gift of God to thee, as sure as thou art born of Adam; nay, hast thou never yet owned him, art thou wandered from him, as far as the prodigal son from his father's house, yet is he still with thee, he is the gift of God to thee, and if thou wilt turn to him, and ask of him, he has living water for thee.

Poor sinner! consider the treasure thou hast within thee, the Saviour of the world, the eternal Word of God lies hid in thee, as a spark of the divine nature, which is to overcome sin and death, and hell within thee, and generate the life of heaven again in thy soul. Turn to thy heart, and thy heart will find its Saviour, its God within itself. Thou seest, hearest, and feelest nothing of God, because thou seekest for him abroad with thy outward eyes, thou seekest for him in books, in controversies, in the Church, and outward exercises, but there thou wilt not find him, till thou hast first found him in thy heart. Seek for him in thy heart, and thou wilt never seek in vain, for there he dwells, there is the seat of his light and Holy Spirit.

For this turning to the light and Spirit of God within thee, is thy only true turning unto God, there is no other way of finding him, but in that place where he dwelleth in thee. For though God be everywhere present, yet he is only present to thee in the deepest, and most central part of thy soul. Thy natural senses cannot possess God, or unite thee to him, nay thy inward faculties of understanding, will, and memory, can only reach after God, but cannot be the place of his habitation in thee. But there is a root, or depth in thee, from whence all these faculties come forth, as lines from a centre, or as branches from the body of the tree. This depth is called the centre, the fund or bottom of the soul. This depth is the unity, the eternity, I had almost said, the infinity of thy soul; for it is infinite, that nothing can satisfy it, or give it any rest, but the infinity of God. In this depth of the soul, the Holy Trinity brought forth its own living image in the first created man, bearing in himself a living representation of Father, Son, and Holy Ghost, and this was his dwelling in God and God in him. This was the kingdom of God within him, and made paradise without him. But the day that Adam did eat of the forbidden earthly tree, in that day he absolutely died to this kingdom of God within him. This depth or centre of his soul having lost its God, was shut up in death and darkness, and became a prisoner in an earthly animal, that only excelled its brethren, the beasts, in an upright form, and serpentine subtilty. Thus ended the fall of man. But from that moment that the God of mercy inspoke into Adam the bruiser of the serpent, from that moment all the riches and treasures of the divine nature came again into man, as a seed of salvation sown into the centre of the soul, and only lies hidden there in every man, till he desires to rise from his fallen state, and to be born again from above.

Awake then, thou that sleepest, and Christ, who from all eternity has been espoused to thy soul, shall give thee light. Begin to search and dig in thine own field for this pearl of eternity, that lies hidden in it; it cannot cost thee too much, nor canst thou buy it too dear, for it is all, and when thou hast found it, thou wilt know, that all thou hast sold or given away for it, is as mere a nothing, as a bubble upon the water.

But if thou turnest from this heavenly pearl, or tramplest it under thy feet, for the sake of being rich, or great, either in church or state, if death finds thee in this success, thou canst not then say, that though the pearl is lost, yet something has been gained instead of it. For in that parting moment, the things, and the sounds of this world, will be exactly alike; to have had an estate, or only to have heard of it, to have lived at Lambeth twenty years, or only to have twenty times passed by the palace, will be the same good, or the same nothing to thee.

* * *

There is but one salvation for all mankind, and that is the life of God in the soul. God has but one design or intent towards all mankind, and that is to introduce or generate his own life, light, and spirit in them, that all may be as so many images, temples, and habitations of the Holy Trinity. This is God's good will to all Christians, Jews, and heathens. They are all equally the desire of his heart, his light continually waits for an entrance into all of them, his wisdom crieth, she putteth forth her voice, not here, or there, but everywhere, in all the streets of all the parts of the world.

Now there is but one possible way for man to attain this salvation, or life of God in the soul. There is not one for the Jew, another for a Christian, and a third for the heathen. No; God is one, human nature is one, salvation is one, and the way to it is one; and that is, the desire of the soul turned to God. When this desire is alive and breaks forth in any creature under heaven, then the lost sheep is found, and the shepherd has it upon his shoulders. Through this desire the poor prodigal son leaves his husks and swine, and hastes to his father: it is because of this desire, that the father sees the son, while yet afar off, that he runs out to meet him, falls on his neck, and kisses him. See here how plainly we are taught, that no sooner is this desire arisen, and in motion towards God, but the operation of God's Spirit answers to it, cherishes and welcomes its first beginnings, signified by the father's seeing, and having compassion on his son, whilst yet afar off, that is, in the first beginnings of his desire. Thus does this desire do all, it brings the soul to God, and God into the soul, it unites with God, it co-operates with God, and is one life with God. Suppose this desire not to be alive, not in motion either in a Jew, or a Christian, and then all the sacrifices, the service, the worship either of the law, or the gospel, are but dead works, that bring no life into the soul, nor beget any union between God and it. Suppose this desire to be awakened, and fixed upon God, though in souls that never heard either of the law or gospel, and then the divine life, or operation of God, enters into them, and the new birth in Christ is formed in those who never heard of his name. And these are they 'that shall come from the east, and from the west, and sit down with Abraham, and Isaac, in the kingdom of God.'

Oh my God, just and good, how great is thy love and mercy to mankind, that heaven is thus everywhere open, and Christ thus the common Saviour to all that turn the desire of their hearts to thee! Oh sweet power of the bruiser of the serpent, born in every son of man, that stirs and works in every man, and gives every man a power, and desire, to find his happiness in God! O holy Jesus, heavenly light, that lightest every man that cometh into the world, that redeemest every soul that follows thy light, which is always within him! O Holy Trinity, immense ocean of divine love in which all mankind live, and move, and have their being! None are separated from thee, none live out of thy love, but all are embraced in the arms of thy mercy, all are partakers of thy divine life, the operation of thy Holy Spirit, as soon as their heart is turned to thee! Oh plain, and easy, and simple way of salvation, wanting no subtleties of art or science, no borrowed learning, no refinements of reason, but all done by the simple natural motion of every heart, that truly longs after God. For no sooner is the finite desire of the creature in motion towards God, but the infinite desire of God is united with it, co-operates with it. And in this united desire of God and the creature is the salvation and life of the soul brought forth. For the soul is shut out of God, and imprisoned in its own dark workings of flesh and blood, merely and solely, because it desires to live in the vanity of this world. This desire is its darkness, its death, its imprisonment, and separation from God.

When therefore the first spark of a desire after God arises in thy soul, cherish it with all thy care, give all thy heart into it, it is nothing less than a touch of the divine loadstone, that is to draw thee out of the vanity of time into the riches of eternity. Get up therefore and follow it as gladly, as the wise men of the east followed the star from heaven that appeared to them. It will do for thee, as the star did for them, it will lead thee to the birth of Jesus, not in a stable at Bethlehem in Judea, but to the birth of Jesus in the dark centre of thy own fallen soul.

I shall conclude this first part, with the words of the heavenly illuminated, and blessed Jacob Behmen.

'It is much to be lamented, that we are so blindly led, and the truth withheld from us through imaginary conceptions; for if the divine power in the inward ground of the soul was manifest, and working with its lustre in us, then is the whole Triune God present in the life and will of the soul; and the heaven, wherein God dwells, is opened in the soul, and there, in the soul, is the place where the Father begets his Son, and where the Holy Ghost proceeds from the Father and the Son.

'Christ says, "I am the Light of the world, he that followeth me, walketh not in darkness." He directs us only to himself, he is the Morning Star, and is generated and rises in us, and shines in the darkness of our nature. O how great a triumph is there in the soul, when he arises in it! then a man knows, as he never knew before, that he is a stranger in a foreign land.'

The Spirit of Prayer
Part Two

THE THIRD DIALOGUE

Rusticus. I have brought again with me, gentlemen, my silent friend, Humanus, and upon the same condition of being silent still. But though his silence is the same, yet he is quite altered. For this twenty years I have known him to be of an even cheerful temper, full of good-nature, and even quite calm and dispassionate in his attacks upon Christianity, never provoked by what was said either against his infidelity, or in defence of the gospel. He used to boast of his being free from those four passions and resentments, which, he said, were so easy to be seen, in many or most defenders of the gospel-meekness. But now he is morose, peevish, and full of chagrin, and seems to be as uneasy with himself, as with every body else: whatever he says is rash, satirical, and wrathful. I tell him, but he will not own it, that his case is this: the truth has touched him; but it is only so far, as to be his tormentor. It is only as welcome to him, as a thief that has taken from him all his riches, goods, and armour, wherein he trusted. The Christianity he used to oppose is vanished; and therefore all the weapons he had against it, are dropped out of his hands. It now appears to stand upon another ground, to have a deeper bottom, and better nature, than what he imagined; and therefore he, and his scheme of infidelity, are quite disconcerted. But though his arguments have thus lost all their strength, yet his heart is left in the state it was; it stands in the same opposition to Christianity as it did before, and yet without any ideas of his brain to support it. And this is the true ground of his present, uneasy, peevish state of mind. He has nothing now to subsist upon, but the resolute hardness of his heart, his pride and obstinacy. These he cannot give up by the force of his reason; his heart cannot bear the thoughts of such a sacrifice; and yet he feels and knows, that he has no strength left, but in a settled

96

hardness, pride, and obstinacy, to continue as he is. – These, I own, are severe and hard words: but, hard as they are, I am sure Humanus knows, that they proceed from the softness and affection of my heart towards him, from a compassionate zeal to show him where his malady lies, and the necessity of overcoming himself, before he can have the blessing of light, and truth, and peace. Though it is with some reluctance, yet I have chosen thus to make my neighbour known both to himself, and to you, that you may speak of such matters as may give the best relief to the state he is in.

Theophilus. Indeed, Rusticus, I much approve of the spirit you have here shown, with regard to your friend, and hope he will take in good part all that you have said. As for me, I embrace him with the utmost tenderness of affection. I feel and compassionate the trying state of his heart, and have only this one wish, that I could pour the heavenly water of meekness, and the oil of divine love, into it. Let us force him to know, that we are the messengers of divine love to him; that we seek not ourselves, nor our own victory, but to make him victorious over his own evil, and become possessed of a new life in God. His trial is the greatest and hardest that belongs to human nature: and yet it is absolutely necessary to be undergone.

Nature must become a torment and a burden to itself, before it can willingly give itself up to that death, through which alone it can pass into life. There is no true and real conversion, whether it be from infidelity, or any other life of sin, till a man comes to know, and feel, that nothing less than his whole nature is to be parted with, and yet finds in himself no possibility of doing it. This is the inability that can bring us at last to say, with the apostle, 'When I am weak, then am I strong.' This is the distress that stands near to the gate of life; this is the despair by which we lose all our own life, to find a new one in God. For here, in this place it is, that faith, and hope, and true seeking to God and Christ, are born. But till all is despair in ourselves, till all is lost that we had any trust in as our own; till then, faith and hope, and turning to God in prayer, are only things learnt and practised by rule and method; but they are not born in us, are not living qualities of a new birth, till we have done feeling any trust or confidence in ourselves. Happy therefore is it for your friend Humanus, that he is come thus far, that everything is taken from him on which he trusted, and found content in himself. In this state, one sigh or look, or the least turning of his heart to God for help, would be the beginning of his salvation. Let us therefore try to improve this happy moment to him, not so much by arguments of reason, as by the arrows of that divine love which overflows all nature and creature.

For Humanus, though hitherto without Christ, is still within the reach of divine love: he belongs to God; God created him for himself, to be an habitation of his own life, light, and Holy Spirit; and God has brought him and us together, that the lost sheep may be found, and brought back to its heavenly shepherd.

Oh Humanus, love is my bait; you must be caught by it; it will put its hook into your heart, and force you to know, that of all strong things, nothing is so strong, so irresistible, as divine love.

It brought forth all the creation; it kindles all the life of heaven; it is the song of all the angels of God. It has redeemed all the world; it seeks for every sinner upon earth; it embraces all the enemies of God; and from the beginning to the end of time, the one work of providence is the one work of love.

Moses and the prophets, Christ and his apostles, were all of them messengers of divine love. They came to kindle a fire on earth, and that fire was the love which burns in heaven. Ask what God is? His name is love; he is the good, the perfection, the peace, the joy, the glory, and blessing, of every life. Ask what Christ is? He is the universal remedy of all evil broken forth in nature and creature. He is the destruction of misery, sin, darkness, death, and hell. He is the resurrection and life of all fallen nature. He is the unwearied compassion, the long-suffering pity, the never-ceasing mercifulness of God to every want and infirmity of human nature.

He is the breathing forth of the heart, life, and Spirit of God, into all the dead race of Adam. He is the seeker, the finder, the restorer, of all that was lost and dead to the life of God. He is the love, that, from Cain to the end of time, prays for all its murderers; the love that willingly suffers and dies among thieves, that thieves may have a life with him in paradise; the love that visits publicans, harlots, and sinners, and wants and seeks to forgive, where most is to be forgiven.

Oh, my friends, let us surround and encompass Humanus with these flames of love, till he cannot make his escape from them, but must become a willing victim to their power. For the universal God is universal love; all is love, but that which is hellish and earthly. All religion is the spirit of love; all its gifts and graces are the gifts and graces of love; it has no breath, no life, but the life of love. Nothing exalts, nothing purifies, but the fire of love; nothing changes death into life, earth into heaven, men into angels, but love alone. Love breathes the Spirit of God; its words and works are the inspiration of God. It speaketh not of itself, but the Word, the eternal Word of God speaketh in it; for all that love speaketh, that God speaketh, because love is God. Love is heaven revealed in the soul; it is light, and truth; it is infallible; it has no errors, for all errors are the want of love. Love has no more of pride, than light has of darkness; it stands and bears all its fruits from a depth, and root of humility. Love is of no sect or party; it neither makes, nor admits of any bounds; you may as easily inclose the light, or shut up the air of the world into one place, as confine love to a sect or party. It lives in the liberty, the universality, the impartiality of heaven. It believes in one, holy, catholic God, the God of all spirits; it unites and joins with the catholic Spirit of the one God, who unites with all that is good, and is meek, patient, well-wishing, and long-suffering over all the evil that is in nature and creature. Love, like the Spirit of God, rideth upon the wings of the wind; and is in union and communion with all the saints that are in heaven and on earth. Love is quite pure; it has no by-ends; it seeks not its own; it has but one will, and that is, to give itself into everything, and overcome all evil with good. Lastly, love is the Christ of God; it comes down from heaven; it regenerates the soul from above; it blots out all transgressions; it takes from death its sting, from the devil his power, and from the serpent his poison. It heals all the infirmities of our earthly birth; it gives eyes to the blind, ears to the deaf, and makes the dumb to speak; it cleanses the lepers, and casts out devils, and puts man in paradise before he dies. It lives wholly to the will of him, of whom it is born; its meat and drink is to do the will of God. It is the resurrection and life of every divine virtue, a fruitful mother of true humility, boundless benevolence, unwearied patience, and bowels of compassion. This, Rusticus, is the Christ, the salvation, the religion of divine love, the true Church of God, where the life of God is found, and lived, and to which your friend Humanus is called by us. We direct him to nothing but the inward life of Christ, to the working of the Holy Spirit of God, which alone can deliver him from the evil that is in his own nature, and give him a power to become a son of God.

Rusticus. My neighbour has infinite reason to thank you, for this lovely draught you have given of the spirit of religion; he cannot avoid being affected with it. But pray let us now hear, how we are to enter into this religion of divine love, or rather what God has done to introduce us into it, and make us partakers again of his divine nature.

Theophilus. The first work, or beginning of this redeeming love of God, is in that Immanuel, or God with us, treasured up, or preserved in the first Adam, as the seed of the woman, which in him, and all his posterity, should bruise the head, and over-come the life of the serpent in our fallen nature. This is love indeed, because it is universal, and reaches every branch of the human tree, from the first to the last man, that grows from it. Miserably as mankind are divided, and all at war with one another, everyone appropriating God to themselves, yet they all have but one God, who is the Spirit of all, the life of all, and the lover of all. Men may divide themselves, to have God to them-selves; they may hate and persecute one another for God's sake; but this is a blessed truth, that neither the hater, nor the hated, can be divided from the one, holy, catholic God, who with an unalterable meekness, sweetness, patience, and goodwill towards all, waits for all, calls them all, redeems them all, and comprehends all in the outstretched arms of his catholic love. Ask not therefore how we shall enter into this religion of love

and salvation, for it is itself entered into us, it has taken possession of us from the beginning. It is Immanuel in every human
soul; it lies as a treasure of heaven, and eternity in us; it cannot
be divided from us by the power of man; we cannot lose it ourselves; it will never leave us nor forsake us, till with our last
breath we die in the refusal of it. This is the open gate of our
redemption; we have not far to go to find it. It is every man's
own treasure; it is a root of heaven, a seed of God, sown into our
souls by the Word of God; and, like a small grain of mustard-seed,
has a power of growing to be a tree of life. Here, my friend, you
should, once for all, mark and observe, where and what the true
nature of religion is; for here it is plainly shown you, that its place
is within; its work and effect is within; its glory, its life, its perfection, is all within; it is merely and solely the raising a new life,
new love, and a new birth, in the inward spirit of our hearts.
Religion (which is solely to restore man to his first and right state
in God) had its beginning, and first power, from the seed of the
woman, the treader on the serpent's head; and therefore all its
progress, from its beginning to its last finished work, is, and can
be nothing else, but the growing power and victory of the seed
of the woman, over all the evil brought by the serpent into human
nature. For the seed of the woman is the spirit, and power, and
life of God, given or breathed again into man, to be the raiser
and redeemer of that first life, which he had lost. This was the
spiritual nature of religion in its first beginning, and this alone
is its whole nature to the end of time; it is nothing else, but the
power, and life, and Spirit of God, as Father, Son, and Holy
Spirit, working, creating, and reviving life in the fallen soul, and
driving all its evil out of it. This is the true rock, on which the
Church of Christ is built; this is the one Church out of which
there is no salvation, and against which the gates of hell can
never prevail.

* * *

Academicus. But now, Theophilus, I beg we may return to that
very point concerning prayer, where we left off. I think my heart

is entirely devoted to God, and that I desire nothing but to live in such a state of prayer, as may best keep me under the guidance and direction of the Holy Spirit. Assist me therefore, my dear friend, in this important matter; give me the fullest directions, that you can; and if you have any manual of devotion, that you prefer, or any method that you would put me in, pray let me know it.

Rusticus. I beg leave to speak a word to Academicus. I am glad, sir, to see this fire of heaven thus far kindled in your soul; but wonder that you should want to know, how you are to keep up its flame, which is like wanting to know, how you are to love and desire that, which you do love and desire. Does a blind, or sick, or lame man want to know, how he shall wish and desire sight, health, and limbs? or would he be at a loss, till some form of words taught him how to long for them? Now you can have no desire or prayer for any grace, or help from God, till you in some degree as surely feel the want of them, and desire the good of them, as the sick man feels the want, and desires the good of health. But when this is your case, you want no more to be told how to pray, than the thirsty man wants to be told, what he shall ask for. Have you not fully consented to this truth, that the heart only can pray, and that it prays for nothing but that, which it loves, wills, and wishes to have? But can love or desire want art, or method, to teach it to be, that which it is? If from the bottom of your heart you have a sincere, warm love for your most valuable friend, would you want to buy a book, to tell you, what sentiments you feel in your heart towards this friend, what comfort, what joy, what gratitude, what trust, what honour, what confidence, what faith, are all alive, and stirring in your heart towards him? Ask not therefore, Academicus, for a book of prayers; but ask your heart what is within it, what it feels, how it stirs, what it wants, what it would have altered, what it desires? and then, instead of calling upon Theophilus for assistance, stand in the same form of petition to God.

For this turning to God according to the inward feeling, want, and motion of your own heart, in love, in trust, in faith of having from him all that you want, and wish to have, this turning thus unto God, whether it be with, or without words, is the best form of prayer in the world. – Now no man can be ignorant of the state of his own heart, or a stranger to those tempers, that are alive and stirring in him, and therefore no man can want a form of prayer; for what should be the form of his prayer, but that which the condition, and state of his heart demands? If you know of no trouble, feel no burden, want nothing to be altered, or removed, nothing to be increased or strengthened in you, how can you pray for anything of this kind? But if your heart knows its own plague, feels its inward evil, knows what it wants to have removed, will you not let your distress form the manner of your prayer? or will you pray in a form of words, that have no more agreement with your state, than if a man walking above-ground, should beg every man he met to pull him out of a deep pit. For prayers not formed according the real state of your heart, are but like a prayer to be pulled out of a deep well, when you are not in it. Hence you may see, how unreasonable it is to make a mystery of prayer, or an art, that needs so much instruction; since every man is, and only can be, directed by his own inward state and condition, when, and how, and what he is to pray for, as every man's outward state shows him what he outwardly wants. And yet it should seem, as if a prayer-book was highly necessary, and ought to be the performance of great learning and abilities, since only our learned men and scholars make our prayer-books.

Academicus. I did not imagine, Rusticus, that you would have so openly declared against manuals of devotion, since you cannot but know, that not only the most learned, but the most pious doctors of the church, consider them as necessary helps to devotion.

Rusticus. If you, Academicus, were obliged to go a long journey on foot, and yet through a weakness in your legs could not set one foot before another, you would do well to get the best travelling crutches that you could.

But if, with sound and good legs, you would not stir one step, till you had got crutches to hop with, surely a man might show you the folly of not walking with your own legs, without being thought a declared enemy to crutches, or the makers of them.

Now a manual is not so good an help as crutches, and yet you see crutches are only proper, when our legs cannot do their office. It is, I say, not so good an help as crutches, because that which you do with the crutches, is that very same thing, that you should have done with your legs; you really travel; but when the heart cannot take one step in prayer, and you therefore read your manual, you do not do that very same thing, which your heart should have done, that is, really pray. A fine manual therefore is not to be considered as a means of praying, or as something that puts you in a state of prayer, as crutches help you to travel; but its chief use, as a book of prayers to a dead and hardened heart that has no prayer of its own, is to show it, what a state and spirit of prayer it wants, and at what a sad distance it is from feeling all that variety of humble, penitent, grateful, fervent, resigned, loving sentiments, which are described in the manual, that so, being touched with a view of its own miserable state, it may begin its own prayer to God for help. But I have done. Theophilus may now answer your earnest request.

Theophilus. Your earnest desire, Academicus, to live in the spirit of prayer, and be truly governed by it, is a most excellent desire; for to be a man of prayer is that which the apostle means by living in the spirit, and having our conversation in heaven. It is to have done, not only with the confessed vices, but with the allowed follies and vanities of this world. To tell such a soul of the innocence of levity, that it needs not run away from idle discourse, vain gaiety, and trifling mirth, as being the harmless relief of our heavy natures, is like telling the flame, that it needs not always be ascending upwards. But here you are to observe, that this spirit of prayer is not to be taught you by a book, or brought into you by an art from without, but must be an inward birth, that must arise from your own fire and light within you, as the air arises from the fire and light of this world. For the spirit of every being, be it what or where it will, or be its spirit of what kind it will, is only the breath or spirit that proceeds from its own fire and light. In vegetative, sensitive, and intellectual creatures, it is all in the same manner; spirit is the third form of its life, and is the birth that proceeds from the other two; and is the manifestation of their nature and qualities. For such as the fire and light are, such and no other, neither higher nor lower, neither better nor worse, is the spirit that proceeds from them. Now the reason why all, and every life does, and must stand in this form, is wholly and solely from hence, because the Deity, the one source and fountain of all life, is a triune God, whose third form is, and is called, the Spirit of God, proceeding from the Father, and the Son.

The painful sense and feeling of what you are, kindled into a working state of sensibility by the light of God within you, is the fire and light from whence your spirit of prayer proceeds. In its first kindling nothing is found or felt, but pain, wrath, and darkness, as is to be seen in the first kindling of every heat or fire. And therefore its first prayer is nothing else but a sense of penitence, self-condemnation, confession, and humility. It feels nothing but its own misery, and so is all humility. This prayer of humility is met by the divine love, the mercifulness of God embraces it; and then its prayer is changed into hymns, and songs, and thanksgivings. When this state of fervour has done its work, has melted away all earthly passions and affections, and left no inclination in the soul, but to delight in God alone, then its prayer changes again. It is now come so near to God, has found such union with him, that it does not so much pray as live in God. Its prayer is not any particular action, is not the work of any particular faculty, not confined to times, or words, or place, but is the work of his whole being, which continually stands in fulness of faith, in purity of love, in absolute resignation, to do, and be, what and how his beloved pleases. This is the last state of the spirit of prayer, and is its highest union with God in this life. Each of these foregoing states has its time, its variety of workings, its trials, temptations, and purifications, which can only be known by experience in the passage through them. The one only and infallible way to go safely through all the difficulties, trials, temptations, dryness, or opposition, of our own evil tempers, is this: it is to expect nothing from ourselves, to trust to nothing in ourselves, but in everything expect, and depend upon God for relief. Keep fast hold of this thread, and then let your way be what it will, darkness, temptation, or the rebellion of nature, you will be led through all, to an union with God: for nothing hurts us in any state, but an expectation of something in it, and from it, which we should only expect from God. We are looking for our own virtue, our own piety, our own goodness, and so live on and on in our own poverty and weakness; to-day pleased and comforted with the seeming strength and firmness of our own pious tempers, and fancying ourselves to be some-what; to-morrow, fallen into our own mire, we are dejected, but not humbled; we grieve, but it is only the grief of pride, at the seeing our perfection not to be such as we vainly imagined. And thus it will be, till the whole turn of our minds is so changed, that we as fully see and know our inability to have any goodness of our own, as to have a life of our own.

For since nothing is, or can be, good in us, but the life of God manifested in us, how can this be had but from God alone? When we are happily brought to this conviction, then we have done with all thought of being our own builders; the whole spirit of our mind is become a mere faith, and hope, and trust in the sole operation of God's Spirit, looking no more to any other power to be formed in Christ new creatures, than we look to any other power for the resurrection of our bodies at the last day. Hence may be seen, that the trials of every state are its greatest blessings; they do that for us, which we most of all want to have done, they force us to know our own nothingness, and the all of God.

People who have long dwelt in the fervours of devotion, in an high sensibility of divine affections, practising every virtue with a kind of greediness, are frightened, when coldness seizes upon them, when their hymns give no transport, and their hearts, instead of flaming with the love of every virtue, seem ready to be overcome by every vice. But here, keep fast hold of the thread I mentioned before, and all is well. For this coldness is the divine offspring, or genuine birth, of the former fervour; it comes from it as a good fruit, and brings the soul nearer to God, than the fervour did. The fervour was good, and did a good work in the soul; it overcame the earthly nature, and made the soul delight in God, and spiritual things; but its delight was too much an own delight, a fancied self-holiness, and occasioned rest and satisfaction in self, which if it had continued uninterrupted, undiscovered, an earthly self had only been changed into a spiritual self. Therefore I called this coldness, or loss of fervour, its divine offspring, because it brings a divine effect, or more fruitful progress in the divine life. For this coldness overcomes, and delivers us from spiritual self, as fervour overcame the earthly nature. It does the work that fervour did, but in an higher degree, because it gives up more, sacrifices more, and brings forth more resignation to God, than fervour did; and therefore it is more in God, and receives more from him. The devout soul therefore is always safe in every state, if it makes everything an occasion either of rising up, or falling down into the hands of God, and exercising faith, and trust, and resignation to him. Fervour is good, and ought to be loved; but tribulation, distress, and coldness, in their season are better, because they give means and power of exercising an higher faith, a purer love, and more perfect resignation to God, which are the best state of the soul. And therefore the pious soul that eyes only God, that means nothing but being his alone, can have no stop put to its progress; light and darkness equally assist him; in the light he looks up to God; in the darkness he lays hold on God; and so they both do him the same good.

This little sketch, Academicus, of the nature and progress of the spirit of prayer, may show you, that a manual is not so great a matter as you imagined.

The best instruction that I can give you, as helpful, or preparatory to the spirit of prayer, is already fully given, where we have set forth the original perfection, the miserable fall, and the glorious redemption of man. It is the true knowledge of these great things that can do all for you, which human instruction can do. These things must fill you with a dislike of your present state, drive all earthly desires out of your soul, and create an earnest longing after your first perfection. For prayer cannot be taught you, by giving you a book of prayers, but by awakening in you a true sense and knowledge of what you are, and what you should be; that so you may see, and know, and feel, what things you want, and are to pray for. For a man does not, cannot pray for anything, because a fine petition for it is put into his hands, but because his own condition is a reason and motive for his asking for it. And therefore it is, that the *Spirit of Prayer*, in the first part, began with a full discovery and proof of these high and important matters, at the sight of which the world, and all that is in it, shrinks into nothing, and everything past, present, and to come, awakens in our hearts a continual prayer, and longing desire, after God, Christ, and eternity.

A Letter to Mr. J.T.

MY DEAR WORTHY FRIEND,

Whom I much love and esteem, your letter, though full of complaints about the state of your heart, was very much according to my mind, and gives me great hopes, that God will carry on the good work he has begun in you, and lead you by his Holy Spirit through all those difficulties, under which you at present labour.

The desire that you have, to be better than you find yourself at present, is God's call begun to be heard within you, and will make itself to be more heard within you, if you give but way to it, and reverence it as such; humbly believing that he that calls, will, and only can, help you to pay right and full obedience to it.

As to the advertisement in the public papers, it deserved no regard from you, or anyone else. It must have come, either from a very ignorant and weak friend, or from a very insignificant enemy to the writings of J.B. But be it as it will, it was not an object of your attention, nor could be of any use to you. J. BOEHME

But to come to your own state, you seem to yourself to be all infatuation and stupidity, because your head, and your heart are so contrary, the one delighting in heavenly notions, the other governed by earthly passions, and pursuits. It is happy for you, that you know and acknowledge this: for only through this truth, through the full and deep perception of it, can you have any entrance, or so much as the beginning of an entrance into the liberty of the children of God. God is in this respect dealing with you, as he does with those, whose darkness is to be changed into light. Which can never be done, till you fully know (1) the real badness of your own heart, and (2) your utter inability to deliver yourself from it, by any sense, power, or activity of your own mind.

And were you in a better state, as to your own thinking, the matter would be worse with you. For the badness in your heart, though you had no sensibility of it, would still be there, and would only be concealed, to your much greater hurt. For there it certainly is, whether it be seen and found, or not, and sooner or later, must show itself in its full deformity, or the old man will never die the death which is due to him, and must be undergone, before the new man in Christ can be formed in us.

All that you complain of in your heart is common to man, as man. There is no heart that is without it. And this is the one ground, why every man, as such, however different in temper, complexion, or natural endowments from others, has one and the same full reason, and absolute necessity, of being born again from above.

Flesh and blood, and the spirit of this world, govern every spring in the heart of the natural man. And therefore you can never enough adore that ray of divine light, which breaking in upon your darkness, has discovered this to be the state of your heart, and raised only those faint wishes that you feel to be delivered from it.

For faint as they are, they have their degree of goodness in them, and as certainly proceed solely from the goodness of God working in your soul, as the first dawning of the morning, is solely from, and wrought by the same sun, which helps us to the noon-day light. Firmly, therefore, believe this, as a certain truth, that the present sensibility of your incapacity for goodness, is to be cherished as a heavenly seed of life, as the blessed work of God in your soul.

Could you like any thing in your own heart, or so much as fancy any good to be in it, or believe that you had any power of your own to embrace and follow truth, this comfortable opinion, so far as it goes, would be your turning away from God and all goodness, and building iron walls of separation betwixt God and your soul.

For conversion to God, only then begins to be in truth, and reality, when we see nothing that can give us the least degree of faith, of hope, of trust, or comfort in any thing, that we are of ourselves.

To see vanity of vanities in all outward things, to loath and abhor certain sins, is indeed something, but yet as nothing, in comparison of seeing and believing the vanity of vanities within us, and ourselves as utterly unable to take one single step in true goodness, as to add one cubit to our stature.

Under this conviction, the gate of life is opened to us. And therefore it is, that all the preparatory parts of religion, all the various proceedings of God either over our inward, or outward state, setting up, and pulling down, giving, and taking away, light, and darkness, comfort, and distress, as independently of us, as he makes the rain to descend, and the winds to blow, are all of them for this only end, to bring us to this conviction, that all that can be called life, good, and happiness, is to come solely from God, and not the smallest spark of it from ourselves. When man was first created, all the good that he had in him was from God alone. N.B. This must be the state of man for ever. – From the beginning of time through all eternity, the creature can have no goodness, but that which God creates in it.

Our first created goodness is lost, because our first father departed from a full, absolute dependence upon God. For a full, continual, unwavering dependence upon God, is that alone which keeps God in the creature, and the creature in God.

Our lost goodness can never come again, or be found in us, till by a power from Christ living in us, we are brought out of ourselves, and all selfish truths, into that full and blessed dependence upon God, in which our first father should have lived.

What room now, my dear friend, for complaint at the sight, sense, and feeling of your inability to make yourself better than you are? Did you want this sense, every part of your religion would only have the nature and vanity of idolatry. For you cannot come unto God, you cannot believe in him, you cannot worship him in spirit and truth, till he is regarded as the only giver, and you yourself as nothing else but the receiver of every heavenly good, that can possibly come to life in you.

Can it trouble you, that it was God that made you, and not you yourself? Yet this would be as unreasonable, as to be troubled that you cannot make heavenly affection, or divine powers to spring up, and abide in your soul.

God must for ever be God alone; heaven, and the heavenly

nature are his, and must for ever and ever be received only from him, and for ever and ever be only preserved, by an entire dependence upon, and trust in him. Now as all the religion of fallen man, fallen from God himself, and the spirit of this world, has no other end, but to bring us back to an entire dependence upon God; so we may justly say, blessed is that light, happy is that conviction, which brings us into a full and settled despair, of ever having the least good from ourselves.

Then we are truly brought, and laid at the gate of mercy: at which gate, no soul ever did, or can lay in vain.

A broken and contrite heart God will not despise. That is, God will not, God cannot pass by, overlook, or disregard it. But the heart is then only broken and contrite, when all its strong holds are broken down, all false coverings taken off, and it sees, with inwardly opened eyes, every thing to be bad, false, and rotten, that does, or can proceed from it as its own.

But you will perhaps say, that your conviction is only an uneasy sensibility of your own state, and has not the goodness of a broken and contrite heart in it.

Let it be so, yet it is rightly in order to it, and it can only begin, as it begins at present in you. Your conviction is certainly not full and perfect; for if it was, you would not complain, or grieve at inability to help or mend yourself, but would patiently expect, and only look for help from God alone.

But whatever is wanting in your conviction, be it what it will, it cannot be added by yourself, nor come any other way, than as the highest degree of the divine life can come into it.

Know therefore your want of this, as of all other goodness. But know also at the same time, that it cannot be had through your own willing and running, but through God that showeth mercy; that is to say, through God who giveth us Jesus Christ. For Jesus Christ is the one only mercy of God to all the fallen world.

Now if all the mercy of God is only to be found in Christ Jesus, if He alone can save us from our sins; if He alone has power to heal all our infirmities, and restore original righteousness, what room for any other pains, labour, or enquiry, but where, and how Christ is to be found.

It matters not what our evils are, deadness, blindness, infatuation, hardness of heart, covetousness, wrath, pride, and ambition, &c., our remedy is always one and the same, always at hand, always certain and infallible. Seven devils are as easily cast out by Christ as one. He came into the world, not to save from this, or that disorder, but to destroy all the power and works of the devil in man.

If you ask where, and how Christ is to be found, I answer, in your heart, and by your heart, and nowhere else, nor by any thing else.

But you will perhaps say, it is your very heart that keeps you a stranger to Christ, and him to you, because your heart is all bad, as unholy as a den of thieves.

I answer, that the finding this to be the state of your heart, is the real finding of Christ in it.

For nothing else but Christ can reveal, and make manifest the sin and evil in you. And he that discovers, is the same Christ that takes away sin. So that, as soon as complaining guilt sets itself before you, and will be seen, you may be assured, that Christ is in you of a truth.

For Christ must first come as a discoverer and reprover of sin. It is the infallible proof of his holy presence within you.

Hear him, reverence him, submit to him as a discoverer and reprover of sin. Own his power and presence in the feeling of your guilt, and then he that wounded, will heal, he that found out the sin, will take it away, and he who showed you your den of thieves, will turn it into a holy temple of Father, Son, and Holy Ghost.

And now, sir, you may see, that your doubt and enquiry of me, whether your will was really free, or not, was groundless.

You have no freedom, or power of will, to assume any holy temper, or take hold of such degrees of goodness, as you have a mind to have. For nothing is, or ever can be goodness in you, but the one life, light, and spirit of Christ revealed, formed, and begotten in your soul. Christ in us is our goodness, as Christ in us is our hope of glory. But Christ in us is the pure free gift of God to us.

But you have a true and full freedom of will and choice, either to leave, and give up your helpless self to the operation of God on your soul, or to rely upon your own rational industry, and natural strength of mind. This is the truth of the freedom of your will, in your first setting out, which is a freedom that no man wants, or can want so long as he is in the body. And every unregenerate man has this freedom.

If therefore you have not that which you want to have of God, or are not that you ought to be in Christ Jesus, it is not because you have no free power of leaving yourself in the hands, and under the operation of God, but because the same freedom of your will, seeks for help where it cannot be had, namely, in some strength and activity of your own faculties.

Of this freedom of will it is said, 'According to thy faith, so be it done unto thee'; that is to say, according as thou leavest and trustest thyself to God, so will his operation be in thee.

This is the real, great magic power of the first turning of the will; of which it is truly said, that it always hath that which it willeth, and can have nothing else.

When this freedom of the will wholly leaves itself to God, saying, 'Not mine, but thy will be done', then it hath that, which it willeth. The will of God is done in it. It is in God. It hath divine power. It worketh with God, and by God, and comes at length to be that faith, which can remove mountains; and nothing is too hard for it.

And thus it is, that every unregenerate son of Adam hath life and death in his own choice, not by any natural power of taking which he will, but by a full freedom, either of leaving, and trusting himself to the redeeming operation of God, which is eternal life, or of acting according to his own will and power in flesh and blood, which is eternal death.

And now, my dear friend, let me tell you, that as here lies all the true and real freedom, which cannot be taken from you, so in the constant exercise of this freedom, that is, in a continual leaving yourself to, and depending upon the operation of God in your soul, lies all your road to Heaven. No divine virtue can be had any other way.

All the excellency and power of faith, hope, love, patience, and resignation, &c., which are the true and only graces of the spiritual life, have no other root or ground, but this free, full leaving of yourself to God, and are only so many different expressions of your willing nothing, seeking nothing, trusting to nothing, but the life-giving power of his holy presence in your soul.

To sum up all in a word. Wait patiently, trust humbly, depend only upon, seek solely to a God of light and love, of mercy and goodness, of glory and majesty, ever dwelling in the inmost depth and spirit of your soul. There you have all the secret, hidden, invisible upholder of all the creation, whose blessed operation will always be found by a humble, faithful, loving, calm, patient introversion of your heart to him, who has his hidden heaven within you, and which will open itself to you, as soon as your heart is left wholly to his eternal ever-speaking WORD, and ever-sanctifying Spirit within you.

Beware of all eagerness and activity of your own natural spirit and temper. Run not in any hasty ways of your own. Be patient under the sense of your own vanity and weakness; and patiently wait for God to do his own work, and in his own way. For you can go no faster, than a full dependence upon God can carry you.

You will perhaps say, Am I then to be idle, and do nothing towards the salvation of my soul? No, you must by no means be idle, but earnestly diligent, according to your measure, in all good works, which the law and the gospel direct you to, both with regard to your self and other people.

Outward good works to other people, may be justly considered as God's errand on which you are sent, and therefore to be done faithfully, according to the will, and in obedience to him that sent you.

But nothing that you do, or practise as a good to yourself, and other people, is in its proper state, grows from its right root, or reaches its true end, till you look for no willing, nor depend upon any doing that which is good, but by Christ, the wisdom and power of God, living in you. I caution you only against all eagerness and activity of your own spirit, so far as it leads you to seek, and trust to something that is not God, and Christ within you.

I recommend to you stillness, calmness, patience, &c., not to make you lifeless, and indifferent about good works, or indeed with any regard to them, but solely with regard to your faith, that it may have its proper soil to grow in, and because all eagerness, restlessness, haste, and impatience, either with regard to God, or ourselves, are not only great hindrances, but real defects of our faith and dependence upon God.

Lastly, be courageous then, and full of hope, not by looking at any strength of your own, or fancying that you now know how to be wiser in yourself, than you have hitherto been; no, this will only help you to find more and more defects of weakness in yourself; but be courageous in faith, and hope, and dependence upon God. And be assured, that the one infallible way to all that is good, is never to be weary in waiting, trusting, and depending upon God manifested in Christ Jesus.

I AM YOUR HEARTY FRIEND
AND WELL-WISHER.

March 20, 1756.